A Hickory Springs Romance ❤

Peaches and Honey

KARMEN LEE

*For anyone who thought going home would be quick,
only to trip over love and a reason to stay.*

When PR executive Honey Parker inherits her late aunt's peach farm and bakery in her sleepy hometown of Hickory Springs, Georgia, she plans a quick sale and a swift return to her high-powered life in Chicago. But the small town with too many painful memories, and the curvaceous, honey-sweet beekeeper next door, might have other plans.

After an accident shattered Mimi Smith's Olympic equestrian dreams, she has spent years crafting her life in quiet harmony by nurturing bees, baking pastries infused with her secret peach honey at the bakery she co-owned with Honey's aunt, and helping train a new generation of girls dreaming of equestrian stardom. When a developer's deal threatens to pave over her passions, she's ready to fight for her home and her heart.

What starts as tension over property lines and

mismatched finances, slowly melts into laughter, shared recipes, and a warmth Honey hasn't felt in years. But when sabotage strikes and old dreams clash with new desires, both women must decide what they're willing to risk for a chance at something real.

Content Notes

Here are a few notes for what you'll come across in this story. No spoilers intended, just so you know what you are getting into. Feel free to skip ahead if you don't want to read over these notes.

This read discusses parental death (prior to the start of the book), cancer, isolation from family, emotional neglect, possible animal cruelty.

Chapter 1

Honey

I knew the second I saw the "Welcome to Hickory Springs" sign, complete with a smiling peach in a cowboy hat, that I'd made a mistake. The sign was the same one from my childhood, paint cracked and peeling, and the peach looked like it was winking at me, which somehow felt like mockery. The late-afternoon sun bounced off the metal letters, stabbing at my eyes, and the first thought that crossed my mind wasn't *nostalgia*. It was, *God, I hate this.* I shouldn't have been here. I should've been back in Chicago, sipping a five-dollar oat milk latte, writing a copy for a new perfume launch and arguing over Pantone swatches with my boss. Instead, I was turning my car down Parker Road, yes, the same Parker that I saw every time I sent an email showcasing my own last name.

Apparently, my family was a *founding family*, which in Hickory Springs meant we got our own street. It would be sort of legendary if not for the fact that no one outside the town knew what the fuck Hickory Springs even was. Or where. No one in my circle, professional or social, knew about the place that I had been born in. Hell, at this point, it had been so long since I was last here that I barely knew anything about it. All I knew was that it had somehow captured me in its grasp once again.

The steering wheel felt slick under my palms, and I forced myself to take a couple of deep breaths. *Fantastic*, I thought. *Anxiety sweats. A perfect way to make a grand entrance to a town where gossip was probably an Olympic sport.* This town wasn't part of my carefully curated future. My mother died when I was five and it was her family who had ties to the town—ties that were severed the moment my father remarried and moved us to Chicago. He'd petitioned to change my last name from my mother's, but apparently five-year-old me had been adamant about keeping the connection to my mom and her family. It was something I was regretting now. He never said it out loud, but it was like he wanted to scrub Hickory Springs right out of me.

My new stepmother, Melanie, didn't exactly

encourage visits to "that dusty little farm," beyond the occasional one-week trek down during summer vacation. Those stopped once I hit high school and spent more time preparing for debate club and taking internships where I could until it was just birthday cards from Aunt Beatrice and the occasional care package—a jar of peach preserves and maybe a knitted scarf that smelled faintly of her signature lavender scent. I kept them for a while, tucked away in my room like contraband, until I got old enough to stop caring. But now Aunt Bea was dead, and I was back, inheriting everything she owned because, as the lawyer told me in his syrupy Southern drawl, "You're the last Parker, Miss Honey." Like it was some grand honor instead of a cosmic fucking joke that I was the last in line of a family I never truly knew.

The road narrowed, bordered by tall pines and hickories—the kind of postcard-pretty trees that made outsiders sigh about so-called country charm. I just felt itchy, and I was glad I had thought to bring my allergy medication. Somewhere up ahead, I spotted the roofline of a white farmhouse, and my stomach knotted so hard I could practically feel it twisting in place. Of course, that was the exact moment my cell phone rang. I slapped the Bluetooth button on my steering wheel and tried not to let the frustration of being back in an unfamiliar place bleed into my tone.

"Hey, Marisol," I said, trying to sound casual even when I felt anything but.

My boss didn't bother with pleasantries. She never did, really. It was one of the things I admired about her even if it did chafe sometimes to be spoken too so bluntly. I always wondered if that was my latent Southern sensibilities at play. "Honey, please tell me you're on a flight home."

I winced as I noted just how far away from an airport I was. "Technically? I'm on a dirt road."

"Honey—"

"In Georgia," I added quickly. "Heading to the farm."

A beat of silence met my words before I heard her sigh. "The farm. Right. Your *heritage* farm." I could practically taste the quotation of the word heritage like a bitter flavor on the back of my tongue. "Look, we need you back as soon as possible. The D'Amour Cosmetics pitch is Monday. Monday, Honey."

I tightened my grip on the wheel. "I don't know if I'll be back by Monday."

"You *don't know?*"

I could hear her manicured nails drumming on her desk. I imagined the disapproving arch of her perfectly maintained brow. I had once asked her, before I realized she despised small talk, where she got her eyebrows shaped. She had given me such a bland look that I quickly made note to never ask her anything that didn't pertain to work again.

"Marisol," I said, trying to figure out a way to put my next words delicately. "I just inherited a whole farm complete with horses, bees, and apparently a bakery. It's...a lot."

"You hate dirt," she reminded me flatly. "And bees."

"Exactly. That's why it's a lot."

I heard her sigh, long and dramatic but not necessarily wrong given the situation. "Two weeks, you said. That was two weeks ago."

"Things changed," I muttered.

"I'll give you one more week, Honey. After that..." She didn't finish the sentence, but the unspoken threat was loud enough. After that, don't bother coming back. I hung up before she could scold me further and decided to blame the cut call on a bad signal.

"Great. Now, I'm getting guilt from work and from the grave." I pressed my head back against the seat and tried to think soothing thoughts, but nothing helped. All I could think about was how much this trip was going to cost me. Hell, it had already cost me money and a frustrating phone call conversation with my father just to get down here.

The driveway to the farm curved like a lazy question mark, gravel crunching under my tires. The house came into view, and I was momentarily struck breathless. It was big and old, with a wraparound porch and white paint that was more tired eggshell than freshly painted white. There were rocking chairs up front that looked as old as the house itself, and wind chimes I could faintly hear as they swayed in the gentle breeze. The whole place looked like something off a postcard, which would've been charming if I chose to be here rather than being forced by legalities and the judgmental whispers of my ancestors.

I parked my car, killed the engine, and stepped out. The air hit me first, thick with the scent of sweet grass and something floral I couldn't place. I swore I could hear bees humming somewhere nearby, a faint buzzing that made the hairs on my arms rise. The place was quiet. Too quiet. It was nothing like my neighborhood back in Chicago where I could always count on seeing someone wander by whether they were from the neighborhood or not. Here, the loudest sound came from the windchimes, and while they were a lot more pleasant than honking cars or yelling people, it all still unnerved me.

I walked onto the porch, the wood creaking under my heels, and called out a quick hello. As expected, no one answered. I snorted softly at myself. "What the hell did you expect? Aunt Bea to walk out like a friendly fucking ghost?"

I shook my head and tried the handle. The front door was unlocked, because of course it was. I was sure crime here was just a suggestion. Back home, I would never dream of leaving any of my doors unlocked for an extended period of time. But here, it must be some sort of prerequisite. When I stepped inside, the smell was the first thing that hit me. There was a faint hint of dust, but also honey, lavender, and the faintest trace of cinnamon, like someone had been baking cookies a decade ago and the scent never left, instead seeping into the very foundation of the house itself. Sunlight filtered through gauzy curtains, painting gold rectangles on the hardwood floor. Every surface had a photo; old sepia-toned ancestors with solemn faces. There was one of my mom as a little girl on the same porch I had just passed by, and one of Aunt Bea holding up a jar of honey with a triumphant smile. It was all so normal and yet nothing about this was. I had never really thought about what would happen if I came back here again. Sure, I figured I would eventually visit, if only to make it up to my aunt for not visiting for the past decade. The last time I had been here was junior year of high school.

Aunt Beatrice had enveloped me in a tight hug practically the moment my plane touched down. I hadn't quite known what to do with that. I could count on one hand the number of hugs I remembered getting from my father. When she had pulled back, her dark brown eyes were suspiciously shiny, but she had only welcomed me in and sat me at the couch with a tray full of cookies and a house worth of stories. Now, she was gone, and the last link I had to this part of my life was legally going to drown me in debt. I was still staring at a family portrait when a voice floated in from somewhere near the house. I nearly jumped out of my skin, ridiculously wondering if haunted houses were actually a thing before I realized the person was clearly muttering to themselves. Whoever they were, they were outside in the backyard. I spun toward the open back door and saw her.

At first, I thought she was some sort of apocalyptic alien complete with full white suit, mesh veil, and gloves. She carried a metal thing in one hand, steam curling out of it like it was a weapon of mass destruction or something. My heart did a weird little stutter, half fear, half...something else. I moved through the kitchen and opened the back door, stepping out onto the back porch in time to see her pull up her veil giving me my first good look at her.

She was beautiful. Not in an airbrushed-magazine type way, but in a strange amalgamation of sun-kissed farm-girl and Nubian-goddess made for worshipping. Dark hair was tucked into some sort of head covering that dipped into her suit, but I could see that her forehead was beaded with sweat. She had a heart-shaped face with cheeks that looked utterly soft and eyes the color of dark chocolate with the kind of confident, unbothered gaze that made me feel like *I* was the intruder even though I technically owned the place.

I blinked. "Who are you?"

She cocked a brow. "Mimi Smith. I run Parker's Peach Farm."

"Parker's Peach Farm?"

"Yes. You know...the farm you're currently on?" She shrugged like it was obvious. "I manage things for your aunt, Bea. Or...managed, I guess. There's the bees, the orchard, the bakery, the horses. Someone had to once she got sick, so we worked out a deal and..."

I opened my mouth when she trailed off as if realizing she was rambling. None of the thoughts in my head managed to work themselves out, so I closed it, then tried again. "I'm Honey Parker."

Her lips twitched into something that was almost a smirk. "Yeah. I know." The way she said it made my name sound both ridiculous and inevitable.

"Well," I said, forcing myself not to feel awkward like I always had when a pretty girl looked at me like I was an alien. "You're trespassing."

Her smirk widened into a full-blown smile—slow, amused, and just this side of infuriating. "I can't trespass on property I co-own."

I blinked again, slower this time. "Excuse me? Co-own?" I thought quickly. None of the conversations I had with the estate planner had mentioned this. "What do you mean, co-own? Are we related?" I really fucking hoped not. This was not some episode of kissing cousins. I would have to bleach my brain if I found out I thought my cousin was cute non-platonically.

"Hardly. I only have a few cousins and none of my family is from here." She unzipped her suit halfway, leaning casually against the porch rail like she had all the time in the world. "Read the letter."

"What letter?"

"The one Bea left for you. It's on the kitchen table in the envelope you probably haven't bothered to open yet."

I bristled at the idea that I hadn't done my due diligence. Being thorough was part of my damn job. "I opened the *lawyer's* letter."

"This one's different," she said as if explaining directions to a small child. "Bea wrote it for you. It'll explain...well, everything."

And then, without another word, she flipped her veil back down, turned, and walked away, the white suit glowing in the sunlight like some kind of infuriating beacon. I stood there, stunned silent and gripping the doorframe. My annoyance bubbled up like soda fizzing over, but I had no one to unleash it on but myself.

"Read the letter," I muttered under my breath, mocking her voice. "What is this, *Pride and Prejudice?* Read the letter, Miss Parker. Ugh."

But even as I rolled my eyes, I watched her disappear into what I assumed were peach trees, the curve of her hips in that ridiculous beekeeper suit doing something unwelcome to my focus. I shook myself, hard.

"Nope. Absolutely the fuck not. You have no time for hot farmers with shitty attitudes." That wasn't exactly a fair assessment. She hadn't been mean, just a bit sarcastic. It had been so long since I last chatted with someone who wasn't a close friend or co-worker that I wasn't sure how to handle someone new. *Fuck, I really need to get out more.*

When I went back inside, I found the envelope on the kitchen table just like she said, my name written in my aunt's familiar looping script. The paper smelled faintly of lavender, like she'd spritzed it with that familiar aroma, and my throat tightened. Despite the years between us, the scent of lavender never failed to make me think of Bea. In what few memories I still had of my mother, she carried the same scent; comforting and soothing even when I was at my angriest as a teen shipped away to a farm and a family I no longer truly knew.

I unfolded it and tried to ignore the ache in my chest.

My dearest Honey—

My eyes burned already, and I paused before reading more. The house was quiet around me and yet it was like there was an energy there welcoming me in. I pulled out the closest chair and sat in it, giving myself time to breathe before diving into the letter again.

I know we haven't been close for a while now and I wish that were different. It would make all of this so much easier, and I'm as much to blame for that as your father.

I shook my head slowly, wishing I could tell her to do away with her misplaced guilt even as I continued reading.

You are the last Parker, and this is your home as much as it was mine and your mother's. I wish I had had more time to introduce you to Mimi. She's been such a treasure helping me run things these past few years, and really, I think knowing her will do you some good. She might not be a Parker in name, but she loves this land, and I know as co-owner, she will keep our legacy's best interests at heart.

I wasn't sure what to think about that, but now I knew why Mimi was here. I wasn't sure why that information wasn't in the packet I had received from the lawyer though. I frowned as I tried to think of a reason it would have been omitted, but when nothing came, I kept reading instead, pledging to solve that mystery later.

I'm leaving you the orchard, the bakery, the hives, the horses—everything. I hope you'll find something here that keeps the memories of your mother and me alive in your heart. I love you, my sweet girl. Please don't ever forget that. Your mother would be so proud of the beautiful, driven woman you've become. Never forget your

*legacy was built on more than just blood
but also love.*

Love always, Bea

I stared at the words until they blurred, then folded the letter carefully like it might break if I breathed too hard. The house creaked around me, the smell of honey thick in the air. Outside, I could see the white blur of Mimi's suit moving between white boxes that I assumed were hives, smoke puffing gently as she worked. I should've been angry. Hell, I was angry. There was so much I still didn't understand. I pressed the letter flat against the table and sighed.

"Well, Aunt Bea," I muttered. "You might've just ruined my whole life."

Chapter 2

Mimi

The air carried the fragrant scent of horse sweat and the faint tang of Georgia red clay. Most folks would probably wrinkle their noses when they got their first drags of that thick mix, but for me, it was the norm. It was a far cry from sterile offices, emails, and the kind of work that left you staring at a glowing screen, wondering if you were alive or just moving your fingers. It was a life I hadn't thought would be possible after my accident, and yet, here I was living my plan B and not being mad at it.

"Sit tall, Lily!" I called out, watching my student bounce unevenly on a shaggy little sorrel pony. The girl was all gangly elbows like a foal that hadn't quite figured out how to move all its limbs in tandem, but her eyes and the way her tongue stuck out spoke to nothing but the type of stubborn determination most only had as a kid. It was a look I remembered well from some of my own photos taken when I was her age. It was why I decided to continue this work. "Pretend you have a crown on your head. Don't let it fall off."

Lily straightened so quickly I almost laughed, her face bright under her helmet and her brown skin glistening with the kind of sweat only Georgia summers could wring out of you. Her braids swung against her back as the pony trotted a wobbly circle, and I jogged along the fence line, my boots sinking into the dusty ground.

"That's it! Heels down. Remember to keep your toes forward. You're not driving your mama's car; you're guiding a horse." She giggled at that, lost her balance for a second, then found it again. Lord, the girl had grit and stubbornness. Horses respected stubbornness and so did I. I tried not to pick favorites out of my few students, but I saw the most potential in Lily and I hoped she would keep at it.

The cicadas had been hollering since three o'clock, filling the hot, heavy air with their static song. Sweat soaked the collar of my t-shirt, and my curls were puffing bigger with every minute. Lily finished her last circle, then slid off the pony, beaming like she'd just won the Kentucky Derby.

"You did so good today," I said, holding up my hand for a high-five. Her palm smacked mine, sticky and warm. "Watch those videos I sent you at home, and practice your posture and counting, and next week, you'll be smoother than me."

Her grin could've powered the lights for the whole farm. "Thank you, Miss Mimi!"

Her mama came up in her sundress and big hoop earrings, fanning herself with the program pamphlet I'd given her last month. "Come on, Lily. Let's get you in the car before you melt."

They left in their SUV, the air conditioning roaring like a jet ready to blast off. I watched them go before leaning against the fence and taking a slow pull from my water bottle. The horizon glowed gold-pink over the peach grove, the trees heavy with fruit. Out here without a horse trotting in front of me, the world smelled like sap and soil. Sweet and sticky in all the best ways. Abruptly, Cassandra's voice carried from the other side of the barn. I rolled my eyes at her noisy appearance, glad that I had already put away the pony, so he didn't get scared off by her charging in like a loose bull with an attitude and a score to settle.

"Well, look at you. Got these kids riding like Olympians already."

I turned, already smiling as Cassandra walked around the barn, her beekeeping suit half-zipped and her veil under her arm. Sweat dotted her temples, but her grin was pure mischief.

"You're late."

"I'm not late," she shot back, peeling off her gloves and tossing them into her veil. "I was being held hostage by a queen bee with an attitude. You know how it is."

"Mm-hmm. Blame it on the bees. It's always the bees."

"They understand me. Unlike some people." She winked. Then her eyes lit up in that nosy-friend way I knew too well. "So, did you meet her yet?"

I sipped my water, buying myself a second even though I knew exactly who she was talking about. "Meet who?"

"Don't play," Cassandra said as she put her free hand on her hip. "Honey Parker. Aunt Bea's niece and prodigal city girl. Half the town has been buzzing about her coming home, and the other half has been speculating if she even truly exists."

The name curled in my chest in a way I didn't care to name. "That's ridiculous. Of course, she exists, and for your information, the answer is yes," I said, careful and slow. "We met earlier this morning when I was checking the hives near the house."

Cassandra's grin spread like soft butter on hot corn-bread. "And?"

"And it was...awkward." When Cassandra kept staring, I continued. "And she was overwhelmed."

"Uh-huh."

"And," I sighed, giving in. "She was as annoyingly attractive in person as she was in her photos."

Cassandra hollered like she'd just won the lottery, laughing so hard she had to brace herself on the barn wall. "I knew it! I knew you were going to say that."

"Don't start," I muttered, heat climbing into my cheeks as I took another pull of water and tried to ignore the memory of Honey in my mind. I hadn't known what to expect when I met her. I had heard the car pull up the driveway and it was a split-second decision that had me making my way back to the house instead of staying out near the hives like I'd originally planned.

"What is she like? Does she have that big-city polished look like she just stepped out of a magazine?"

"Maybe," I admitted, rolling my eyes. "But I didn't take a picture or anything, if that's what you're about to ask."

Cassandra gasped dramatically. "You mean to tell me you didn't sneak one little photo of the new woman in town? Not even a quick phone snap? Mimi, I'm disappointed in you. An attractive woman strolls into your life, and you didn't even think to get evidence that she actually exists?"

"That's creepy," I said flatly, though I couldn't help the way my lips curled up at her antics.

She wagged a finger. "It's only creepy if you hide it. If she posed for you, that's called romance."

"Cass."

"What? I'm just saying." She gave me that sly look. "You're curious about the woman. Admit it."

I focused on sipping from my water bottle and ignoring her entirely too astute of a question. Honey Parker had shown up looking like she owned the whole state of Georgia with her model-sharp cheekbones, sleek permed hair that clearly fought humidity for shits and giggles, and clothes that screamed money. When she'd accused me of trespassing on land I co-owned, I'd wanted to argue and laugh in equal measure.

"She's Aunt Bea's niece," I said, as if that explained everything. "That's all."

Cassandra arched an eyebrow and hummed. "Well, I can't wait to meet her myself."

"You might not have to wait long," I murmured as the crunch of tires on gravel reached my ears signaling Honey's return to the house. I had heard her take off about an hour after she'd come in, and I was curious about where she had gone despite it not being any of my damn business.

Cass darted to the barn door like she was in a spy movie. "Speak of the devil."

My stomach dipped at her entirely too enthusiastic response. I knew it was novel to get new people coming into town, but I also knew her excitement was more about my reaction to Honey's presence and less about Honey herself. "Don't make it weird."

"Me?" Her grin widened as she glanced at me over her shoulder. "I'm subtle as sweet tea."

"Your sweet tea is diabetes in a glass."

"I don't know what you're talking about," she said, turning her nose up at me.

That was the biggest lie I'd heard all week, but I didn't feel like calling her on it just yet. I waited for her to store her things and dropped off my own. We walked back to the house together, pausing by the back door to take off our shoes and leave them on the porch before walking in. The kitchen was cool when we stepped inside, and the air carried faint notes of flour and vanilla. Bea's kitchen had always smelled like this —like something was either baking, cooling, or waiting to be tasted. It still lingered even though she'd been gone now for a month. I swallowed hard at the reminder that I wouldn't come downstairs in the morning and see her at the stove crafting one of her signature dishes before heading to the bakery to open up.

"You okay?" Cassandra asked softly. When I looked over at her, her eyes were on me with understanding and concern clear in their brown gaze. I smiled though I knew it looked watery.

"Yeah," I said before taking a moment to breathe. "It's just so weird that she's gone, you know?"

Cassandra wrapped an arm around my shoulders and leaned her head against mine. "I know. I have a bag of her biscuits in my freezer that I can't bring myself to thaw out because once they're gone..." She paused and I wrapped an arm around her waist. "She was so cool for an old lady."

That choked a laugh out of me. "She would have smacked you upside the head for calling her that." I sniffled softly before shaking my head. "Let's start some dinner."

This was a comforting routine Cassandra and I had started doing just before Bea's passing. If not for knowing the land ownership still needed to be settled, I would have asked her to move in just so it wasn't only me in a house clearly meant for a large family. I grew up in a large residence, but it had never seemed that way with my older brother, Alonso, always making himself known and my younger sister, Cady, stomping around refusing to be ignored or left behind. I'd just set the knife down when the stairs in the hallway creaked. Cassandra's elbow found my ribs, sharp enough to make me hiss, and then she looked back to the stove like she wasn't two seconds from losing her mind with glee.

When footsteps went from the stairs to just outside

the kitchen, I turned and almost lost my breath. Honey was in the doorway and gone was the high-gloss city armor she'd shown up in earlier. She was no longer wearing her blazer or heels. Instead, she wore black yoga pants that clung like sin, a tank top that revealed toned brown shoulders, and her hair pulled back into a ponytail so sleek it looked like it had its own PR manager. I was not prepared for her to look even better dressed down and I was even less prepared for how my body responded to it.

"Evening," she said. Her voice was cool and practiced, like she was used to walking into rooms and setting the vibe. I recognized the tone well though it had become less familiar the more time I spent in Hickory Springs far removed from the formal parties I'd grown up with.

"Evening." I nodded and tried not to let my gaze linger for longer than would be proper. "Did you find a room to settle into?"

She leaned against the doorframe, arms crossed. That should've looked defensive, but on her, it looked like a magazine spread. The soft light from the window caught the gold in her skin, highlighted the curve of her cheekbone and the way her plush lips pressed together like she was holding back either a smile or a complaint.

"Yes. There were a few more rooms than I was expecting."

I nodded again, feeling a little like a bobble head but unable to keep myself from doing it. "Bea's room was downstairs, and I haven't..." I paused thinking about how her room was exactly as it looked the last time she was in it. It had seemed disrespectful to move anything, so I hadn't. I knew eventually I'd have to go in there if only to help Honey figure out what to do with everything, but I wasn't ready yet. "I'm glad you found one that will work for you."

"Thank you."

Behind me, Cassandra coughed into her fist. Which was her version of *don't make it weird* but sounded suspiciously like *you're making it weird*.

"We were just making dinner," I blurted, words tumbling out like marbles I couldn't catch. "Do you want to join us?"

Her eyes flicked toward the stove, where onions hissed in the pan, filling the kitchen with their sharp, sweet smell. For one long second, I imagined her saying yes. I imagined her sliding onto one of the stools, ponytail swishing as I set a plate in front of her, while Cassandra gave me looks behind her back. But that thought fizzled away when she shook her head.

"Thanks, but no. I'm headed into town to pick up a few things I'll need while I'm here."

The words were simple and her tone neutral, but still, my stomach dipped. I found myself disappointed despite knowing it was a long shot. Honey didn't know me beyond what little Bea might have told her. Silence filled the kitchen, awkward as could be. The fridge hummed like a bass note only broken up by the sound of oil popping in the skillet. Even so, the rapid thump of my heartbeat in my ears drowned out both.

"Another time, maybe," I managed, trying for casual and probably landing at desperate. I hadn't been this tongue-tied in front of a woman since boarding school when I first learned where my desires lied. I wasn't known as being a charmer, but I could do better than this. "I would be more than happy to show you around the farm and apiary as well."

Honey gave a nod. It wasn't a big one; just a small dip of her chin, but somehow it felt like a verdict. Then she pushed off the frame, turned, and walked out without another word. I swear, I didn't plan to watch her leave. Still, I couldn't help but notice the way her ponytail swung, how her yoga pants left *nothing* to the imagination, and how she moved like she owned every inch of space she stepped into. But I'd be hard-pressed to lie about how my gaze lingered at the doorway, straining to catch just one more glimpse of her.

The door clicked shut and I was rooted to the spot. Honey's car started and then there was the sound of gravel crunching under tires as she pulled away from the house. It was ridiculous, but I couldn't help but focus on that sound until it completely faded away.

Thirty-one is too damn old to be having a crush. The thought didn't keep me from wondering though. I jerked in surprise when Cassandra let out a long, low whistle. I had almost forgotten she was here. When I looked over at her, she was fanning herself with a kitchen towel. When she saw me watching her, she shook the towel at me.

"Girl. You were holding out on me."

"What are you talking about?" I asked with a confused frown.

She cocked an eyebrow at me before putting a hand on her hip. "Seriously?"

"What?" I snapped, too quick and sharp to hide the way my heart was beating faster than it should have been.

Cassandra gave me an incredulous look. "What do you mean 'what?' That woman is fine with a capital 'F'. You severely undersold the eye candy that is now gracing us with her presence."

I scowled at her for a moment before grabbing a tomato like I was about to commit murder by vegetable. "I didn't undersell anything." My tone was defensive, but I couldn't do anything about that now. "And don't you even think about flirting with her. It wouldn't be appropriate."

Cassandra snorted before going back to stirring the onions like she hadn't just set the kitchen on fire with that comment. "Why not? You said you weren't interested, and I have been a saint the past few months. I deserve a pair of legs wrapped around my shoulders, especially legs as nice as hers."

"Because she's here to grieve her aunt," I hissed, chopping the tomatoes too hard. Juice spattered my arm, and I paused with a sigh. "Because she hasn't lived here in years and is probably counting the days till she leaves. And because..."

I stopped, the words sticking like honey at the bottom of the jar.

"Because you're already lookin' at her like she's the last peach in July," Cassandra finished, smug as ever. I glared but all she did was grin back like my expression didn't even phase her. "Don't worry friend. I won't go poaching in your territory."

I wanted to shoot down her words, but I paused. It was probably better for her to think I wanted something with Honey, if only to keep her from going on the prowl. It was for the best that I let her think that I called dibs despite how false that was. I wasn't interested in Honey for any reason other than how things would shake out for the farm. Even if she was gorgeous in a way I hadn't expected. Bea had talked about Honey for years, always with this wistful pride that had left me curious long before today. I had hoped meeting her once would satiate that curiosity and yet, now, I was even more so.

And Lord help me, I knew that meant trouble.

The house was too quiet. It was the first thing I noticed when Cassandra finally left with her to-go container of leftovers, blowing me a kiss over her shoulder like she hadn't just stomped all over my nerves the entire night. The screen door squeaked shut, then the sound of her car faded down the gravel road until nothing remained but the crickets and the lonely creak of my bedroom ceiling fan. After a damn good shower that felt heavenly on my aching back, I flopped on my bed and blew out a breath. I should've been exhausted. The day had been long, heavy with sweat and honey and the ache of missing Bea in every corner. My body should've collapsed the second I hit the mattress, but even when I turned off the overhead light, sleep wouldn't come.

I laid flat on my back, staring at the ceiling shadows like they held answers. The air smelled faintly of lavender from the candle on my bedside table that Bea had given me last spring. It was a smell that tugged at my chest and made my eyes burn with each flick of my eyelids. Normally, the familiar scent soothed me. Tonight, it only sharpened the ache that was accompanied with the ache in my lower back. My head wasn't filled with lavender-scented memories or the long list of chores waiting at dawn. No, my head was filled with *her*.

Honey had walked into the kitchen like she owned the place. She had made her presence known in a way that made it feel natural even if she held herself a little awkwardly. In another life, I could see her there leaning against Bea's old doorframe with her arms folded, cool as you please as Bea tittered around her. I'd spent the last few years in that kitchen, chopping onions and kneading dough on that counter, but somehow, she had fit herself into the space like she'd been carved into it. Like it was her birthright. Hell, I guess it was.

And those damn yoga pants. I could still see the curve of her hips and feel the heat climbing up my neck when she'd tilted her head, considering my invitation with that unreadable expression. I groaned, dragging the pillow over my head like it could smother the memory. It didn't work of course. If anything, the darkness just made the image sharper. Behind my eyelids, I could see her mouth pressed tight like she was holding something back and I swore I could hear her voice, smooth but tired, like honey stirred into tea after a long day.

I rolled onto my side, curling up like I could make myself smaller than the thoughts crowding me. It wasn't just attraction. That would've been easy to shove down, the same way I'd shoved down plenty of things before. No, what rattled me was how fast it all tangled together—the grief for Bea, the weight of the farm's future, and the sudden presence of a niece Bea had loved so much, a niece who looked like every reason I should keep my distance.

I thought of Bea's laugh, soft and musical, carrying through the kitchen on Saturday mornings. She used to stand right by that stove, flipping biscuits, talking about Honey like she was something golden. "That girl's gonna do big things," she'd say, pride shining in her eyes. "She's sharp as a tack and just as beautiful, too. She got my sister's smile. I know she'd be so proud if she could see her."

I'd always nodded, half-listening, too busy pulling pans out of the oven or wiping flour off my arms. I'd never said it out loud, but I'd wondered how Bea could talk about her like she was perfect if she never visited? Why did she have so much pride for someone who lived states away, and barely ever called? But then today happened, and somehow, I understood. There was something magnetic about how Honey carried herself. She walked into the room and the air shifted. It was the type of appeal that made people stop and take notice. I know I had. If Alonso could see me now, he would have already started trying to play matchmaker, and I probably would have let him. Honey was temptation wrapped in soft cotton and sleek ponytail, standing in my kitchen with the ghost of Bea's voice still hanging in the walls.

I sat up, pressing my palms to my eyes until stars flared behind them. This farm was what I needed to focus on. Not her. Except that wasn't simple either. The future loomed, heavy as a storm cloud. The bees were restless this season, the hives temperamental after so much rain. Bakery orders and training the new staff we'd hired a couple months ago kept me up late. Without Bea's steady hands, sharp memory for numbers, and ever-present calm when things got messy, I felt like I was paddling a canoe with my fingertips.

There were debts Bea had refused to let me take care of and repairs that had been put off too long. Thankfully, I had been able to hire more seasonal help for the land that needed tending faster than I could manage with my own two hands. I had stretched myself thin over the past month, but even thin had limits. And I knew Honey probably had no desire to stick around. She would maybe help sort through Bea's things, then she'd leave, back to Chicago where the air smelled like ambition instead of honeysuckle and rain. I shouldn't care.

But I did. The Parker Farm had become my sanctuary and even though it was Honey's legacy, it was also my home. I laid back down, pressing my cheek to the quilt Bea had made for me as a present for my first year being here. The fabric was soft under my skin, and I snuggled into it. My chest hurt, heavy with too many feelings. I thought of Bea's hands, warm despite the tremor of weakness in them as they rested over mine.

"You'll be fine, Mimi," she'd said, her voice a soft song that continued to echo in my mind. "You might not be a Parker in name, but you're one in heart. Trust that."

I sighed before rolling onto my side. The ceiling fan continued to hum as it twirled, and I closed my eyes when I heard the sound of tires coming up the driveway. Crickets chirped outside the window as the night pressed close around me, thick and sticky.

"Lord, don't let me make a fool of myself," I whispered. But deep down, I worried I was already halfway there.

Chapter 3

Honey

The first thing I learned about Hickory Springs was that apparently time worked differently here. Not in a science fiction type of way, but more in the way a town could look like it hadn't changed since I was five years old, and yet somehow still feel brand new. The second thing I learned was that no matter how much time passed, I was still the kid everyone apparently remembered, even if I couldn't return the favor by calling anyone by their name. The third was that this place was a little bigger than I thought.

For some reason, I had decided to traipse into town and get the lay of the land. Main street was easy enough to find, but there were more turns than I was expecting for a small town. Somehow, I ended up at the entrance of another farm before I turned around and decided to use my GPS. Still, it was better than sitting in that house that was so full of barely-there memories of times that I would never get back. It was like the walls were aflutter with whispers of judgement for me being gone so long. I wanted to say it wasn't my fault that I hadn't truly been back to visit in years, but the truth was I could have come back long ago. I was an adult and hadn't been under my father's thumb for a long while. The only thing keeping me away was myself and now I was here and there was no one to welcome me. Well...that wasn't exactly true. There was Mimi. But that brought a whole new set of problems that I also didn't want to deal with.

There was only so much staring at unfamiliar walls a person could do before the silence started chewing on their nerves. And besides, I needed groceries and more toiletries than I had brought down with me. There were only so many dry crackers and questionably old cans in Bea's pantry, and if I was going to survive a few weeks in this place while everything got settled, I needed real food. I also needed a full belly if I was going to brave another conversation with Marisol about how a week wouldn't be long enough to get things done here. It was that thought that drove me from the house and the offer of a meal that smelled delicious and a woman who looked just as good as whatever was being sauteed on the stove.

Mimi was attractive, that much was undeniable. She was the perfect height with dark brown skin that just looked like it smelled like heaven. Where I had the hint of curves that hadn't been fully utilized, hers were fully there and made my palms itch to press against. Attraction wasn't new for me, but it normally didn't come on this strongly this quickly. Truthfully, I didn't have much time for romance. Usually, I went out on the weekends when the need was too much to ignore, and I just needed to touch and be touched. But those encounters typically lasted one night and then never again. I didn't often invite repeats back to my bed because I didn't want feelings to get involved. I had a plan for my life, and I was well on my way to moving into a higher role and gathering the experience and connections I needed to then open my own marketing agency and work for myself.

I flicked on my blinker when the tinny voice of the GPS told me to turn. With a sigh of relief, the main part of town came into view. I knew Walmart loomed across town, relegated to the fringes and out of sight from the main area, and for a second, I considered pulling into its parking lot. It was safe and anonymous; a place with rows upon soulless rows of everything I could need complete with bright fluorescent lights and nobody asking questions. But something in me, maybe stubbornness or maybe masochism, decided if I was back in Hickory Springs, I might as well go all in and act like a local.

I continued down Main Street until I spotted the Cox Family Grocery sign hanging a little crooked but bright like it had been recently repainted. I turned in and decided to treat this like a little adventure. I had never been to an actual family-owned grocery store. Typically, I ordered my groceries to get delivered from one of the big grocery stores on my app and called it a day. I never really thought too hard about groceries. Getting them was just a chore that needed to be done, and I rarely thought about who was getting them for me outside of making sure to tip well, especially if there were substitutions that had to be made to the order.

When I pulled in, the parking lot was half-empty. I wondered if that was because most people were already at home cooking. The building looked exactly like the kind of grocery store that belonged in an old movie with its big front windows, a couple of rocking chairs off to the side like someone might sit there and whittle stories all day, and a door that probably squeaked every time it opened. Sure enough, when I pushed on the door, it squeaked and I couldn't help but shake my head and smile. It probably should have been annoying, but I found it strangely charming. As soon as I walked in, the smell hit me first. My senses were filled with the scent of ripe peaches, fresh bread, and something smoky like hickory wood and barbecue. It smelled like someone cared about food and wanted to entice you into caring about food, too. I stood just inside the doorway a second too long, taking it all in and trying to decide where to even start. I should have made a grocery list, but I was too focused on just getting out of the house, which was my first mistake.

"Honey Parker? Lord, I knew that was you!"

The voice carried across the store like a cannonball, and before I could duck back out and make my escape, an older woman was hustling toward me. Her hair was that perfect shade of all over silver and cut into a short bob that framed her face perfectly. She wore a floral blouse that screamed 'church potluck' and when she hugged me, she smelled faintly of gardenias.

I blinked quickly when she finally pulled away and tried to catch my breath. "Hello." Unsure of what else to say, I waited for some clue as to who she was and why she knew my name.

The woman clapped her hands together like I was a celebrity returning for my hometown tour. In a way, I guess I was, but I was more confused than anything. "I'd know that face anywhere. You look just like your mama, Lord rest her soul."

Cue my stomach flipping as I tried to decide if that statement was a compliment or landmine? It definitely felt like a landmine considering whenever my step-mother mentioned that fact, it was usually when I was doing something that had greatly displeased her. Nothing good in my house had ever come from me looking or acting too much like my mother, so I was unsure of how to take it here.

"Oh," I said, which was about as eloquent as I could manage on such short notice. "Thank you. I wasn't aware that you knew my mother."

"Of course, I knew your mother. Everyone knew Angeline," she announced, beaming like she'd hit it big and was collecting her prize. "I'm Evelyn Turner. Me and your Aunt Bea used to play cards every Thursday night. She always beat me, but I let her, you know. Couldn't stand to see her frown. And you—Lord, I remember when you were just knee-high, running around that farm like you owned the place."

I tried to smile politely, but something about being told I looked like my mom—my dead mom, who I barely remembered except in the few dreams I remembered when I woke up—felt like someone had poked a bruise I'd been ignoring for years. I really wanted to move on, but without really knowing who this woman was, I couldn't think of a good way to redirect the conversation.

"I'm so sorry about Bea," Evelyn went on, her smile softening into something sad. "She was one of the best people I've ever known. I don't remember seeing you at the town gathering. I know she always mentioned not wanting a big funeral."

And there it was. The guilt bomb. I opened my mouth. Closed it again. Because what could I say? That I'd been too busy? That I was overseas for work and hadn't found out until after Bea was already gone? How should I explain to someone I didn't know that the last funeral I ever went to was my mom's back when I still didn't understand that she wasn't going to get up and come back home? Even after finding out about Bea, I hadn't been able to bear walking into a gathering of unfamiliar faces where everyone knew me and I knew no one.

"I—" I started, but mercifully, the universe sent me an escape route.

"Evelyn!" Someone called from the speakers on the wall. "Your pastries are ready at the counter."

Evelyn turned, clapping her hands. "Well, I best be going."

Suddenly, I was wrapped in a cloud of gardenia perfume, Evelyn squeezing me like I was still that five-year-old she remembered. I patted her back awkwardly, then watched as she bustled off down the aisle. I took a deep breath and decided to grab a basket before I got roped into another impromptu reunion with someone else whose face I didn't recognize.

Blessedly, I didn't see Evelyn again as I made my way down the aisle hanging tight to the wall and glancing around to try to seem busy. There were also rows of produce that looked almost too perfect to be real. I picked up apples and bananas for a quick breakfast before continuing down the aisles. The store itself was cozy with shelves stacked with what looked to be local products. There were jars of preserves labeled in neat handwriting, some of the labels familiar from the farm signs I passed on the way to town. I grabbed a loaf of bread and a small carton of milk before pausing when I saw jars of honey that had Bea's farm's name on it. I stared at the honey jars longer than I meant to. Each golden swirl caught the light, and all I could think of was *her*.

Mimi in that damn beekeeper shouldn't have been as eye-catching as she was. It was hard for me not to admire the way her voice had been low and steady, not cowed by my normal countenance at all. She was infuriatingly distracting and annoyingly attractive. I shoved the thought away and continued on. As I walked the aisles, little memories crept in like weeds between cracks in the sidewalk. The smell of cinnamon reminded me of Bea baking cookies when I was young enough to still be persuaded with a sweet treat. The squeak of a cart wheel sounded like the old one she used to push me in before I grew too big to fit in it. By the time I made it to the small deli in the back of the market, I was almost lost in a sea of half-realized memories.

I exhaled slowly, then realized someone else was watching me. Behind the deli counter stood a woman about my age with her hair covered by a mesh cap and an apron tied snug around her waist. She grinned when our eyes met, and her smile was disarming enough to knock some of the stiffness out of my shoulders.

"Hey there," she said, her voice warm. "Miss Evelyn mentioned she saw you in here. Hopefully she didn't talk your ear off too much. She likes to collect people. It's kind of her hobby."

I let out a laugh that sounded rusty even to my own ears. "I figured."

The woman leaned forward on the counter. "I'm Tasha. We were in the same kindergarten class, I think."

Oh. Crap.

"Oh, uh—" I winced when I couldn't think of what to say. How the hell I became a PR executive when I couldn't figure out how to talk to the people in front of me now was anyone's guess. I didn't understand why it was so difficult to talk to people here. Maybe I was just tired from the drive. "Sorry, I don't…"

She waved her hand as if dismissing my inability to

string together a simple sentence. "Don't worry about it. You moved away the summer right after, so I wouldn't expect you to remember every kid you sat next to. I just remember you because your name was Honey, and I thought that was the coolest thing ever. I begged my mama to let me change mine and cried for days after when she said no."

I laughed again, easier and more genuine this time. "Well, thanks for not holding it against me."

Tasha grinned wider. "Never. And hey—welcome back. First trip to the market since you've been here?"

I glanced down at the random menagerie of food in my basket. There really wasn't any rhyme or reason to what I had grabbed. I was really just trying to get my head on straight before heading back home where the memories waited. "Yeah. I needed to grab some food before I started gnawing on furniture."

She reached under the counter and pulled out a paper bag. "Then you need one of these. It's a peach turnover from the bakery. On the house."

"Oh, you don't have to."

"I insist," Tasha replied with a wide smile. "Call it a 'welcome home' gift. I buy more of them than I really should, but I can't help it. I try to give some of them out when people come by."

Something twisted in my chest, sharp and sweet. I

took the bag carefully, like it might bite. "Thanks," I murmured.

She nodded. "Anything else you need, whether it's sliced meat or someone to show you around, you just holler. I left town after high school so I know how jarring it can be to come back and have everything and nothing be the same."

I smiled, for real this time, at such an accurate description of how I had been feeling since I landed. "Thanks Tasha. I appreciate it." She nodded and I said my goodbyes before wandering off into the aisles to see what else I could grab. By the time I made it to the checkout, my chest felt tight with things I couldn't quite name. Outside, the air hit, still hot and humid, making the fabric of my shirt stick to my skin. I loaded my groceries onto the backseat, slid behind the wheel, and let my forehead drop to it for just a moment.

This town is going to eat me alive.

Right on cue, my phone rang and I groaned when I saw Melanie's name. I wasn't in the mood to have a conversation with her right now. I just wanted to drive a little more before getting back to the house and crashing face first into a pile of pillows. Even so, I knew ignoring her would be just as pointless as ignoring my father's call. They never took no response as a response, instead calling repeatedly until I was worn down and answered without hesitation.

"Hello," I said, my voice flat.

"Honey! How are things in Georgia?" Her voice was syrupy, like she thought cheer could cover up the sharp edges underneath.

"Fine."

"Good, good. Have you made progress on finding a buyer for the farm?" The question was expected, but still made me sigh.

I stared out the windshield, watching a kid pedal by on a too-small bike, his shoelaces flapping with each turn. "Not yet."

"Well, don't wait too long, sweetheart. You know your father and I think it's best you sell quickly. Land like that is just so hard to maintain when you aren't there full time, and I know trying to manage it from Chicago would be such a pain. It's probably just better to let it go and put those funds towards settling down back home."

Her words pressed heavy, like she was talking about more than land, and I tightened my grip on the phone. She and my father had been pressing me for months about buying a place in Chicago instead of continuing to rent. They had a point of course. Rental prices had started to get out of hand these days, even with increasing my budget. Still, something had always kept me back from committing to property even after living there for as long as I had. "I'll keep that in mind."

"Wonderful. And do keep us updated, won't you? I know your father misses you."

"Sure. Look, Melanie, it's getting late and I have a busy day tomorrow meeting with the lawyer in town." I didn't really, but I wanted to get off the phone and try to wrap my brain around everything I needed to get done in the next week. "There's paperwork I need to look over so I can be prepared when I go in."

"Oh, of course, of course. You take care, sweetie."

I hung up before she could say more, the silence in my car more agreeable to me after the unwanted conversation. It's not like I hate Melanie. She was fine as a person, generally speaking. She just always either was too involved or not enough. Even after living together for nearly a decade, we never seemed to be able to find a happy medium with our mutual existence. She had become easier to deal with once I'd moved out, but only just.

I sat there a minute, staring at the grocery bags in the rearview mirror. The little paper sack with the peach turnover was on top, and for some reason, it caught my attention. I reached for it then, gripping it tightly before setting it on the passenger seat. I wasn't hungry, but it still represented something to me. It was kindness without expectations and I could use some of that right now.

Chapter 4

Mimi

For a few seconds after opening my eyes, I thought Bea was still alive. I stared at the window for a few minutes trying to understand why I didn't hear her moving around downstairs. The morning light still stretched golden and hazy across my bed, warming me. The sheer curtains on the window still did nothing to keep out the rising sun that often drove me from my sheets. And yet, for some reason, this morning, I was so sure I would hear Bea come tapping on my bedroom door with a mug of hot tea in one hand and a reminder to get up before the world moved on without me.

The first time she had woken me up this way, I had giggled for hours after. It was so different from how I grew up. Even now, I could almost hear her humming, off-key and yet somehow perfect as well as the creak of the floorboard right outside my door that always gave her away. Then my alarm went off. The sound was shrill and all too real, but it snapped me out of that dream space between sleep and awake. I blinked quickly, and just like that, awareness flooded me.

Bea was gone.

I let out a long breath before pressing the heel of my hand to my eyes. Mornings were the hardest. It wasn't that I cried much anymore—I'd done plenty of that the first few weeks—but it was the way her absence felt like a skipped beat in a song I used to know by heart. Everything still looked the same. The house mostly still smelled the same and the farm overall sounded the same...just quieter. I turned over on my back and stared at the ceiling for another thirty seconds before my phone started buzzing on the nightstand beside my bed. I didn't have to glance over to know exactly who it was.

Group chat: *The Smith Bunch.*

My family's idea of checking in had always been to send memes, morning greetings, and daily updates that ranged from the profound, **"Got offered extra peaches at the market!",** to the ridiculous, **"Your daddy says he's making chili tonight and I don't trust him."**

Sometimes the messages didn't even make sense by the time I got them, and I had to stumble through several earlier threads to get an inkling of what was happening. Still, it was a welcome distraction this morning, so I grabbed the phone and eagerly thumbed the chat open.

> Mom: Good morning, baby. Don't forget to take the vitamins I sent you 🤍
>
> Pop: Rise and shine, superstar.
>
> Alonso: Got those beeswax candles you were talking about. They helped me not stress about this upcoming fundraiser, so thanks!
>
> Baby sis: Morning, Buzz Queen! Have a BEE-YOU-tiful day!🐝

I snorted at that last one. Leave it to my baby sister, Cady, to come up with the nickname that refused to die.

> Me: Morning, y'all. Trying not to sting anybody before 9 a.m.

The little hearts and laughing emojis rolled in, one after another, and the tightness in my chest loosened just a fraction. They'd all loved Bea too. She'd pretty much been everybody's aunt, the kind of woman who showed up at birthdays with jars of honey and unsolicited advice, then stayed late to help with the dishes. The first time I had brought her to meet my family,

Cady asked if I'd bagged an older sugar mama and Bea had laughed until I thought she might rip her stomach apart. She'd winked and told them she was too old to try keeping up with someone half her age before launching into a story about her and the mailman having a love-hate relationship due to the number of bills he dropped off at the farm daily. We'd all been on the edge of our seats and Bea had immediately found her place amongst us.

They got it. They understood why I stayed even though Bea was gone and that helped. If not for Bea wanting to be cremated and her ashes spread along her favorite tree line, I think my parents would have given her a plot right beside them in our family mausoleum. I know they had a picture of her in the family estate and already planned donations to the town in her honor. It made me feel a little better that my family recognized how special Bea was as much as I had. She had given me something to work for after my accident and a kind ear when I felt rage so visceral that I worried it would frighten my family. If I could have taken on her illness as my own, I would have in a heartbeat.

With a sigh, I slowly pushed myself to sit, wincing when I felt the familiar tightness in my back. I breathed deep and focused on moving slowly and correctly, going through my morning stretches until most of the stiffness leached from my frame. When I finally got myself out of bed and my feet hit the worn wood floor, a wave of emptiness washed over me so thick I had to grab the dresser for balance. The smell of honey and lavender clung faintly to my pajama shirt—one of Bea's old ones I refused to stop wearing. I pulled it off and folded it neatly before starting my morning routine on autopilot. After a nice hot shower, I pulled on my denim shorts and a loose blouse before making my way out of the room. It was easier to pretend I was fine when I looked put together.

Downstairs, I moved through the hallway and toward the kitchen, intending to start coffee before heading out to check the hives—except the scent of brewed coffee hit me before I even reached the doorway. I froze, frowning in confusion before I remembered I wasn't alone in the house anymore.

Honey.

She was sitting at the kitchen table with her laptop open and a mug of black coffee half-empty beside her. Her posture screamed all business with her back rigidly straight and her jaw tight as she stared at the screen in front of her. She focused like the world depended on her next keystroke, and it was impressive if not a bit terrifying. Even her outfit, a pair of perfectly fitted black slacks and a cream blouse, felt more like a statement piece rather than actual comfortable clothing. Her hair was pinned back neatly into a bun that looked like it could survive an F5 tornado. She didn't notice me at first, though I made no attempt to sneak in unnoticed.

Then again, maybe she did and just didn't care. Either way, the sight of her hit me like a jolt—half irritation, half something else I didn't want to name.

"Good morning," I said finally, because manners were the only weapon I had left in my arsenal before my morning coffee.

She looked up, eyes wide as her fingers stilled on the keyboard. "Oh. Good morning."

We stared at each other a beat too long, like we were both trying to decode what, exactly, we were doing here. Her gaze flickered back to her laptop when it made a chiming noise, and I felt like I could suck in a breath again. Honey was intense in a way Bea never was, and it was interesting to notice their similarities in features and yet not in countenance.

"Have you eaten?" I asked, reaching for a pan even though I wasn't hungry yet. I found that keeping my routine in the morning kept me from spiraling into thoughts that didn't need to be given energy. Sometimes I would head out to the bakery early, but I was trying to practice letting go a little more and trust the people I hired. I didn't want them thinking that I was watching over their shoulders just to catch them slipping up. That wasn't the type of place Bea nor I had wanted to run.

Honey shook her head, eyes flicking back to the screen again. "No. I'm fine."

"Are you sure? I can make—"

"I'm not hungry," she said quickly, then added. "I apologize. I'm just working on an important project with a hard deadline and I'm a bit behind. Pretend I'm not here."

That would've been easier if she weren't sitting right there looking like she belonged in a glossy magazine spread titled *Effortlessly Intimidating Women Who Don't Have Time for Your Awkward Lesbian Shit.*

"Right," I muttered. "Pretend you're invisible. Got it."

I went about my business, frying eggs and toast like I wasn't acutely aware of her in my periphery. Every little sound she made—the soft click of her nails against keys and her softly muttered words as she worked on whatever was on her screen—settled under my skin. At one point, I caught her rubbing her temple, brow furrowed as she glared at the laptop like it personally offended her. The edge of her nails grazed her hairline like she was fighting off a headache which I wouldn't be surprised about given how she occasionally clenched her jaw.

I almost asked if she was okay. Almost. I wasn't

trying to get my head chewed off by the woman I needed to work with to settle the farm and bakery ownership with. Getting on her bad side didn't seem like the best way to have an amicable future partnership or convince her to let me buy her out. Before I could do something ridiculous like ask how she types with those nails, my phone rang, its sharp buzz cutting through the quiet. Hillary's name flashed across the screen, and I sighed in relief at having something else to focus on before connecting the call.

"Hey, Hillary, what's up?"

"Mimi—sorry, I know it's early," Hillary blurted out, her voice nervous and tinny through the line. "There's a man here at the bakery asking questions about...selling and I don't know how to answer him about any of it."

"Selling what?"

"The bakery."

I froze. "What?" My voice came out shriller than I had planned and I glanced at Honey before angling my body and lowering my voice so it wouldn't carry so much. "Sorry. Tell me exactly what he said and don't leave anything out no matter how off topic it seems."

She started talking, her voice speeding up as she clearly got more agitated and worried. "He said he heard rumors about the property being up for sale. I told him I didn't know anything, but he's been waiting around asking about the owner now that Bea...isn't here. And I didn't know what to do, so I called you."

"Good. You did perfect, Hillary. Don't tell him a thing," I said sharply before turning off the stove. Breakfast would just have to wait. "I'll be right there."

"Okay."

"Good job calling me first," I said, wanting to make sure she knew I wasn't upset at her. "You handled everything exactly as you should, and I'm proud of you. Go on back behind the counter and if he asks you anything else, tell him the owner is on her way."

Once she agreed, I hung up, shoving my phone in my pocket. When I turned back toward Honey, she was watching me with a curious look in her gaze.

"Is there a problem?" she asked, tone polite but detached.

"Nothing I can't handle," I said, which was true, but also not the point. I hesitated, then grabbed a mug and poured in hot water from the kettle. I stirred in a spoonful of peach honey and dropped in a chamomile tea bag. The scent rose immediately, sweet and calming. I walked to the kitchen table and set it down beside her laptop.

Her brows knit. "What's that?"

"For your headache."

She blinked slowly looking down at the mug before

looking up at me with slightly wider eyes. "I didn't say I had a headache."

"No," I said, meeting her eyes. "But you were rubbing your head the same way Bea used to when she felt a headache coming on. She always swore by this tea-honey combination. Said it could fix anything except heartbreak and bad posture."

Something flickered across Honey's expression then, something small and uncertain, but before she could respond, I was already walking out the door. I knew I overstepped, but I couldn't help myself. It was clearly a flaw I needed to work on if I was going to be living with Honey for the foreseeable future.

The drive to the bakery took no time at all, but it was still long enough for my irritation to solidify into a righteous, simmering anger. Selling the bakery? Someone really had the audacity to stroll into town and sniff around my place like it was a foreclosed property? Not fucking happening. When I walked into Bake My Day, the man in question was leaning against the counter, talking animatedly at Hillary, who looked like she wanted to melt into the pastry case.

"Can I help you," I said, stepping up to him and fixing him with a cool gaze.

He turned, his smile as fake as bad veneers in a too small mouth. "You must be Mrs. Smith."

"It's Ms.," I said, correcting him. I already didn't like him, and I wanted him out as soon as possible. "And you are?"

"My name is Tom Bennett. I work with a development firm in Macon. We're looking to revitalize some of the properties in Hickory Springs; you know, give this little town a more modern touch. This little bakery has real potential."

I crossed my arms and speared him with a look. "It already has potential. And customers." I glanced around at the people sitting and chatting inside. A couple of them looked over at me curiously and I smiled slightly to reassure them.

He chuckled, though the sound held little humor. He glanced around, his expression showcasing how little he was impressed. "Sure, and this place is charming in that old school kind of way. But what I'm talking about is thinking bigger; maybe a coffee franchise that expands to a second location. With the right group of investors and capital—"

"This bakery isn't for sale," I interrupted, not wanting to hear his pitch deck. I knew how these people worked and I hated it with a passion.

"Everything is for sale," he said, still smiling, though I could see the cracks in it as he looked me over. I'm sure I could guess what he thought he saw. Small town woman with raggedy jean shorts and a blouse covered in peaches. I didn't exactly scream money and that was by design. Only Bea had known that the money I came from was substantial. It was one of the few things we argued about when she refused to let me invest more into the farm itself rather than just fronting the bakery enough to get it off the ground.

"Not this," I said, stepping closer, lowering my voice to the kind of tone I usually reserved for wasps that got too near the hives and men who couldn't take the hint that we liked our cats the same way. "You need to leave."

Something in my face must've convinced him, because the smile faltered. He tugged at his tie as his expression went pinched. "You can't stop progress, Ms. Smith."

I tilted my head and gave him a cool smile. "Watch me."

He hesitated another second before grabbing his briefcase and muttering something about small-town stubbornness. I calmly walked him to the door, holding it open with an exaggerated smile. He huffed again, sounding like a discontent cow before exiting and disappearing down the street.

"Good fucking riddance," I muttered before closing the door. When I turned back, Hillary was hovering behind the counter, wide-eyed and looking like she might have a panic attack at any moment.

"I'm so sorry," she said quickly. "He came in right during the morning rush, and I didn't know what to say—"

"Hey, no. You are totally fine. You did exactly what you should've," I said, softening my expression to reassure her that none of my anger lied with her. "You called me. That's all I ask."

Relief washed over her face. "I didn't want to mess things up."

"You didn't." I smiled. "You handled it fine. We've just had a few vultures circling lately since... They probably heard rumors about the farm and just assumed that the bakery is also up for grabs."

"Is it true?" she asked, curious. "Is the farm being sold?"

I hesitated. "That's complicated." It rattled me that I didn't have any firm answers. I would have bought the farm years ago if Bea had let me. But she had been stubborn to a fault, and I could understand it. Her family had been in Hickory Springs for generations. Selling to an outsider would have probably left her haunted by the ghosts of every ancestor that still stuck around to watch the family continue.

Hillary nodded. I reassured her again, and with a small, relieved smile, she went back to arranging croissants. I slipped into the back room that had been acting as my office, shutting the door behind me. The scent of flour and sugar still hung heavy in the air even with the door closed. I sank into the chair at my desk, where the paperwork waited—leases, supply invoices, and now, unfortunately, the estate documents with Honey Parker's name printed neatly in the corner.

I stared at it for a long minute, tapping my pen against the table. She'd been in the kitchen this morning like she belonged there. Like she wasn't the girl who disappeared for years and now owned half my life. I didn't know whether I wanted to throttle her or kiss her and ask her to stay forever.

I leaned back in my chair, staring at the ceiling. "Bea, why'd you have to go and make things so complicated?"

Chapter 5

Honey

I didn't expect the tea. Honestly, I didn't expect much of anything from the woman who I had mistakenly called a trespasser less than twenty-four hours ago. The morning had been a struggle as I tried to force productivity out of myself like it was a physical workout. My head had started pounding by the third email I'd fielded about this project that wasn't even supposed to be my responsibility to begin with. It was like Marisol was punishing me for daring to have something else going on outside of just work. I know I hadn't helped that. Over the years, I had become the one who volunteered to stay late or join projects without being asked. At first, it was a way for me to get experience and move up the ladder, but even though I was now in an executive-level position, I was still doing it. Some people called me a team player and expressed admiration, but I was feeling less than enthusiastic about it all.

I sighed and sat back in my chair, letting my posture collapse a bit. The steaming mug of chamomile tea sitting beside my laptop caught my attention again. I leaned forward and looked down at it. The honey was still swirling lazy golden ribbons at the bottom, and I focused on that as I took a deep breath.

I noticed the faintest sticky circle under the mug where Mimi set it down. The whole thing was like proof of her existence. For a moment, when I woke up, I had thought I was still in Chicago and that Mimi was just an apparition that my lonely mind made up. When she had stepped into the kitchen, my attention was immediately on her and those damn jean shorts that hugged every curve of her shapely hips. I'd had to practically glare at the computer screen to stop myself from staring. I looked at the mug for a long moment, unsure what to do with the lump in my throat. I hadn't had someone make me tea since—well, since Bea.

When I was a kid before my dad remarried and we moved to Chicago, one of the few memories I had was Aunt Bea making the same tea for me whenever I had any kind of ache. It could have been a scraped-up knee, an upset stomach, or just me having a bad day. She'd pull down the honey jar like it was a holy relic.

"You can fix almost anything with a spoonful of sweetness, baby girl."

I could almost hear her saying it now as I leaned over and breathed deep inhaling the sweet notes from the honey and the chamomile. Sometimes in my memories, it wasn't Bea, but my mom curled up with me on the couch, fragrant tea in one hand and a book in the other. I was never really sure if it was more a hallucination than a memory, but I still took comfort in it.

The thought hit me hard. I hadn't thought about my mom in years, not like this. Not with the smell of honey and chamomile wrapping around me like a blanket I didn't ask for. I swallowed hard before picking up the mug and taking a sip.

"Damnit."

It was perfect. Not too sweet and now not too hot since I'd let it sit before picking it up. It was warm enough to heat me from the inside as the liquid slid down my throat. I didn't need to be getting sentimental over tea; especially when I still had a mess of paperwork to handle and a job to get back to as soon as possible. Still, I couldn't quite stop the way my chest ached.

I was halfway through the cup when my laptop pinged with a new email, and before I could even open it, my phone started ringing. I looked at the screen and sighed. I knew I needed to talk to the estate attorney handling everything, but I really wasn't in the mood. Still, I needed to get this all handled so I braced myself and answered the phone.

"This is Honey."

"Ms. Parker! Good morning." His voice was chipper, and it made me grimace. It was the kind of tone people used when they were about to give you bad news but were hoping that saying it in an upbeat fashion would soften the blow. "I'm glad I caught you. I just sent over a follow-up email, but I wanted to touch base directly."

"Sure," I said warily before sitting back in my chair. "What's going on?"

"Well, I've been reviewing some of the paperwork your aunt filed before she passed. There are a few...developments I wasn't initially aware of when we spoke last week."

That sounded like lawyer code for brace yourself, this is about to get complicated, and I was *not* in the mood for complicated right now.

"What do you mean?"

"Well, I was wondering if you could come down to the office today," he continued. "It'll be easier to explain in person."

His vagueness irked my soul, but I tried to keep it from bleeding into my voice. There was no point in getting irritated with him and it was generally best practice to not piss off the person in charge of your legal future regardless of what they were handling for you. "Is there a problem?"

He hesitated before answering. "Nothing that can't be fixed. Just some...nuances to the property ownership we should clarify."

Fan-fucking-tastic. Because that's exactly what I wanted right now, more nuances.

"I'll be there in twenty," I replied before hanging up and wondering if there was a spell I could learn that could bring Bea back immediately, so I didn't have to deal with all this for a little longer.

Downtown Hickory Springs was about as small-town picturesque as it got. The square was quaint and lined with tidy brick buildings that looked like they'd been plucked straight out of a postcard or one of those Hallmark movies that always came out around Christmas time. It was disarmingly charming, and I hated how much I liked it all. Especially because the last time I'd really seen it, I'd barely been four and holding my mother's hand while watching Aunt Bea wave to every single person who passed by as we made our way to shop after shop. It was the last good memory I had of my mother before her diagnosis and death. It was the last time I really remembered being happy.

Now, decades later, I could still pick out faint pieces of that memory: the smell of baked bread, the lazy flap of the old town flag above City Hall, the faint chime of the church bells from down the road. It was the kind of town that probably still closed on Sundays and hosted festivals for things like choosing a peach queen or something else equally wholesome.

I parked in front of a narrow redbrick building that read *Miller & Brown, Attorneys at Law,* and took a deep breath before stepping inside. The waiting room wasn't exactly what I expected. It smelled like coffee and lemon cleaner, which wasn't out of the norm, but it was far more casual and cozier than I was expecting. The walls were a neutral eggshell with pictures of what looked to be the town decades ago if the coloring was to be believed. There were a couple chairs against one wall and a comfy looking couch against another with a small coffee table between them. I ignored them and went to the counter instead to check in. The receptionist looked up and smiled politely before waving me to go on back, and I nodded my thanks.

Russell's office was filled with more paper than air and I had to keep my eye from twitching when I saw a stack that looked like a piece of architecture ready to fall over. He stood when I came in, smiling like a man who'd had too much caffeine, and immediately I was even more on edge. "Ms. Parker! Thank you for coming on such short notice."

"No problem," I said, though it was absolutely a problem.

He gestured for me to sit on one of the chairs in front of his desk and then walked back around to shuffle through a stack of documents. "I'll get right to it. As we finalized the initial estate documents, I realized there were some secondary filings your aunt completed a few months before her passing. She'd restructured ownership of certain portions of the farm."

I frowned, trying to understand what he was saying. "Restructured how?"

"Well..." He pulled out a large, folded map and spread it across his desk. "As it stands, you are now the primary inheritor of the Parker homestead—the main house, the horse stables, and the peach grove. However, your aunt co-owned several other sections of the property with Ms. Smith—Mimi Smith, that is."

My stomach sank. Of course. Because why wouldn't this entire situation get even messier? Mimi had mentioned co-ownership, but I thought maybe she just meant pieces of equipment that could be easily turned over. I didn't realize she quite literally meant the land itself.

Russell kept going, clearly oblivious to the storm brewing in my expression. "Specifically, Ms. Smith holds joint ownership over the apiary—the bee pastures—and several surrounding acres. Bea sold off other smaller parcels over the years, likely to keep the farm financially stable."

He flipped to another folder, pulling out more pages. "Additionally, there's the matter of Bake My Day."

I blinked. "Bake My what? What the hell is that?"

"It's the bakery. Well, partly your bakery to be precise. It's technically held in a trust for a nonprofit organization—one that, incidentally, your aunt helped found."

My mind was reeling, and I was trying my damndest to keep up with all the information Russell was throwing at me at once. I wasn't surprised that the farm was having financial difficulties. But I hadn't expected all of this. "What kind of nonprofit?"

He smiled faintly, clearly pleased to have an answer. "It's called *Hickory Hearts Collaborative*. From what I've gathered, it provides vocational training and mentorship for young women in the community. The founder and current director listed here—" he turned the page and tapped it "—is Ms. Smith."

"Mimi."

"That's correct," he replied with a nod.

I sat back in the chair, my mind spinning. Bea hadn't just left Mimi a share of the property. She'd tied her into nearly every part of it. The bees, the land, the bakery, even a nonprofit. And somehow, I was tangled in all of it.

"Did my aunt ever mention any of this before?" I asked, though I already knew the answer.

Russell gave a polite wince. "Not to me, no. But I suspect she had her reasons. From what I understand, she and Ms. Smith were very close partners in managing the farm's day-to-day affairs."

"Partners," I repeated, the phrasing tickling my brain in ways that I wasn't happy with. "Are you saying Bea and Mimi were lovers?"

He coughed into his hand. "No, not at all. I meant partners in the business sense, of course." I narrowed my eyes, and he leaned forward, rushing to explain further. "Just between you and me, it was well-speculated that Bea and the mailman, Henry, had a decades long courtship going, though they never confirmed it themselves."

"Right," I replied, still giving him a look. I wasn't sure what emotion was winning in my chest. I was confused by all of this new information and more than a little jealous at the fact that Mimi got to enjoy such a close relationship with the aunt I never really got to reconcile with. Guilt and shame wiggled their way into my chest and burrowed in like termites eating away at my calm. I needed to get out of here and fast.

"I've printed copies of all the relevant deeds, the nonprofit filings, and the trust documentation," Russell said, sliding a thick folder toward me. "Take your time reviewing them, and when you're ready, we can discuss next steps. There's no rush."

"Thank you," I said automatically, though my head was pounding. I was going to need more than a measly cup of tea to combat the pressure that was building in my skull. I gathered the papers, thanked him again, and walked out into the blinding mid-afternoon sun.

The air smelled like warm asphalt and something sweet, but none of it was soothing. I breathed deeply trying and failing to force myself into some semblance of calm. I could only hope that Mimi wasn't anywhere near the house when I got back. I wasn't in the mood to be civil.

I was halfway to my car when a man's voice called out to me. "Ms. Honey Parker?"

I stopped, startled at being called by name in the middle of the sidewalk. I turned in time to see a tall man in a pressed gray suit approaching me. His thin lips were stretched with a smile that didn't quite reach his eyes. His hair was slicked back too neatly, and his shoes looked too expensive to be wandering around in a small town like this.

"Yes?" I said carefully, fixing my stance in case I needed to make a quick getaway. I knew people boasted about the safety of small towns, but I wasn't taking any chances.

"Apologies for coming up to you out of the blue," he said smoothly, extending a hand. "I'm Charles Denton. I believe you're the new owner of the Parker farm?"

"Yes," I said, slowly. "Why?"

"I represent a buyer with an interest in your property. I'd love to discuss potential offers when you're ready."

He held out a business card so crisp it could've sliced bread. I stared at it, not taking it right away. Every instinct I had screamed caution. No one else had approached me like this, and it put me on edge. He didn't seem like a Hickory Springs native and something about that had me wanting to turn and walk the other way.

"How did you know who I was?"

His smile widened just a little too much. "Small towns talk, Ms. Parker. And good opportunities don't stay secret for long." He gestured to the card he was still holding out. I finally accepted it if only to end the conversation.

"I'm not really at the point where I'm seeking offers."

"Of course," he said smoothly. "But should that change, my number is there. We specialize in sustainable redevelopment. Hickory Springs is due for some modernization, wouldn't you agree?"

"I don't think I'm the right person to ask about what Hickory Springs needs," I replied truthfully. I hadn't lived here in years, so how the hell would I know what would and wouldn't be good for the place. Just because the name on the street sign matched mine, didn't mean I had some sort of special insight into the town.

"Progress waits for no one," he said lightly. "Have a good day."

He walked away before I could come up with a better retort, leaving me standing there with the faintest trace of cologne and unease hanging in the air. I glanced down at the card, noting his name and the name of his company: Denton Development Group. The logo was metallic and modern, everything Hickory Springs wasn't. I slipped it into my bag before frowning as I thought back to the impromptu conversation.

I didn't like that he knew my name and I really didn't like that he insinuated the farm was up for sale before I had even listed it. *But isn't that what you plan to do?* I ignored the question and continued to where I'd parked, not stopping until I was safely ensconced in my vehicle. I started the car and tried to not focus on the folder from Russell that sat heavy in the passenger seat. I could feel the weight of Aunt Bea's secrets pressing against me. The farm wasn't just a farm—it was a patchwork of legacies, promises, and, apparently, paperwork.

Right in the middle of it all was Mimi Smith, my so-called co-owner, beekeeper, and the only person who'd managed to make me tea exactly the way I liked it. I gripped the steering wheel, the ghost of honey still sitting heavy on the back of my tongue.

"I don't know who you are, Mimi," I grumbled as I pulled out of my parking spot. "But we need to sit down and have a very serious conversation."

Chapter 6

Mimi

I always said Bake My Day smelled like cinnamon and stress by the time I flipped the sign to 'closed', and today was no exception. Every part of me was exhausted. I wasn't sure if it was because physically today had been difficult or if it was everything else compounding. Probably both.

"Is it okay if I head out, Ms. Mimi?"

I looked up and saw Hillary standing there with her bag on her shoulder. She looked as tired as me and I knew she would be happy to finally get off her feet, as would I. There was a tub with a bottle of Epsom Salt waiting for me when I got home.

"I told you to just call me Mimi," I replied with a tired smile. "But of course. Be careful getting home and I'll see you tomorrow."

She nodded and I kept my smile up until she disappeared down the sidewalk. Only once she was gone did I let it drop. My back twinged a little when I bent to grab the dustpan from the floor and I winced. "Definitely going to need that salt bath," I grumbled to myself as I finished shutting the front lights off and walking over to the counter so I could finish going over some numbers. I was halfway through counting when my phone started buzzing on the counter. I didn't have to look at the screen to know it had to be one of my siblings. They had taken to tag-teaming me during closings in the guise of just wanting to chat while in rush hour traffic. I knew they were both full of shit, but it was sweet...usually, so I let them persist.

I hit answer and put it on speaker. "This better be important."

"It always is," my older brother, Alonso, replied with laughter clear in his voice.

I snorted. "If you're calling to ask me again whether the shipment of cinnamon rolls you begged for is in the mail, the answer is still no. I don't ship pastries and there are plenty of bakeries around the city you can go to without inconveniencing me."

"Wow. I call to check on my sweet little sister, only to be met with such unearned hostility. My heart has truly been broken."

"You don't have a heart," I said, rolling my eyes though I couldn't help but smile at his antics. "You donated it to the foundation years ago. Tax deductible."

His laughter was bright and familiar, and it warmed me after a day of spiraling thoughts that I had tried to keep hidden from Hillary. "Okay, okay, you win. But seriously, Mimi, how are you doing?"

There it was. The question that lived under every conversation we'd had since Bea died. I leaned my hip against the counter, fingers tracing the edge as I went with my standard answer. "I'm fine."

Alonso made a noise—the same snort-groan combination he always made when he didn't believe something I said and he wanted to make sure I knew he didn't. "Mimi."

"Alonso."

"Be honest," he said, exasperation clear in his voice. I almost felt bad about it, but he was the one who called me. I wasn't going to make it easy for him.

"I *am* being honest," I replied. "I'm fine. I'm working and mentoring like I was before. I'm not wallowing or hiding away from the world."

He hummed softly, another familiar sound that meant he was considering saying something he knew I probably wasn't going to like but knowing him he was going to say it anyway. "You know the family would really love for you to come back home. Mom and pop both worry about you and so does Cady. She's talked about delaying her trip out to Texas in case you decide you need to come back home."

I sighed. "That's ridiculous. I'll text her later and tell her not to put off plans because of me."

"It's not just that, and you know it." His voice grew soft and serious, and it made me groan silently. He was getting serious now and I couldn't just brush him off when he acted his age. He was usually so unserious about most things to the point that when he was finally serious about something, the rest of us paid close attention because it was usually extremely important. I didn't like that he was using that against me now. I couldn't just ignore him when he got like this.

I heard him sigh before he spoke up again. "Look, we'd feel better with you close. And I really do have a position lined up for you at the foundation. A good one and not one of those useless positions where you draw a paycheck for transforming oxygen into carbon dioxide. You'd basically be running the community impact program, which as we already know, you'd be great at."

Even as I chuckled at his ridiculousness, I still balked at the idea of settling into a position that I hadn't earned and only got by virtue of coming from the right set of parents. I swallowed and tried to keep my tone light. "I know. And I appreciate it. Really. But I'm good here. Happy, even."

"Really happy?" he asked skeptically. "Is that

genuine or are you pretending because you're too stubborn to admit you'd rather be home, and you think I'll make fun of you for moving back home at your big age?"

I huffed. "It's real you asshole. Plus, you're older than I am and you are in the city, so you don't have a leg to stand on."

"Uh-huh. But I don't live at the homestead Buzz Queen, so it doesn't count."

"And besides," I added, ignoring the nickname that refused to die. I decided to push more and tease him back. The opportunity to have him be the one flustered was too delicious to pass up. "You only want me back so you can steal Cassandra from me."

He choked so loudly I wished I'd been recording. "What are you talking about, Mimi? That is deeply rude. I am offended that you consider my offer anything but coming from the love I have for you as my sister. Deeply hurt. Aggrieved even."

"I'm sure you are." I grinned. "You've been texting her. She told me."

"So? Cassandra's my friend."

"She was *my* friend first."

He scoffed. "Oh please. We share friends just like we share DNA in this family."

"Mm-hmm. And does friendship also explain why you keep pushing for me to at least come visit home and maybe even bring 'a friend' like you don't know exactly which one I would bring with me?"

A guilty silence met me and if not for the ambient noise coming over the phone line, I might have thought Alonso hung up.

"I mean...you could bring another friend if you want. But I know Cassandra would fit in well with our family."

I cackled when he broke. "I knew it. I knew you wanted to get with her, you hussy."

"I hate you," he said, but fondly. "And for the record? Cassandra is nice to look at, yes—"

"Ha!"

"But," he continued pointedly, "I really do miss you and I worry a lot about you which, as the only big brother in the family, I am allowed to do."

My laughter softened into something that prickled uncomfortably behind my ribs. "I know, Alonso and believe me when I say, I love you for it. But I really am okay, even if some days are harder than others."

There was another pause then, but it wasn't as tension-filled as before. I think we had said what we both maybe needed to say about the subject. Right now, going back home wasn't an option for me and I didn't know if it ever would be. I liked Hickory Springs. I liked the slow pace and the friendliness. I even occasionally enjoyed the gossip and how the most mundane of situations could be turned into reality-tv worthy moments. But most of all, I liked the land and the little life I had built here over the past five years.

He cleared his throat as if sensing the shift in the conversation. "How's your back?"

I stretched without thinking and winced. "Sore. Nothing dramatic. I've been doing the exercises Dr. Rawlins gave me and they help."

"And are you finally sleeping like a normal person or are you still staying up too late, prowling around like a thief in the night?"

I pursed my lips at the designation. "Define normal." He sighed but I pretended not to hear it. "It's been a rough month with the will being read and Honey showing up abruptly. Give me a break."

"Mhm," he said slowly. "Speaking of Honey..."

I knew exactly what that tone meant and I wasn't trying to entertain it. It wasn't the first time Alonso or anyone in my family had asked about Honey. Mostly, the questions were about the legal aspects of the foundation and the land ownership. But I had told them who she was, and I knew from Cady's subsequent group texts that they had looked Honey up and probably deduced that, at least physically, she was very much my type.

I needed to put a stop to this direction of the conversation before it even started. "No."

"You didn't even let me—"

"And I won't be," I said, cutting him off.

"But you don't even know what I was about to say." I could hear laughter in his voice, but I didn't buy the innocent act for one second. Alonso was a fucking menace especially when he thought there was someone I might be looking at in more than a platonic sense. He got the same way the last time I talked about liking someone and the time before that. Hell, he kept giving me advice about making a move on Cassandra when he first heard about her and didn't stop until I invited her to visit with me and he saw how she was more of a sister to me than anything else.

"Oh, I'm sure I could guess."

He snorted. "Cady said she's cute and frighteningly accomplished in the PR world."

I rolled my eyes so hard they nearly swung to the back of my skull. "Of course, Cady did. And I'm sure Honey is very accomplished. She certainly seems that way." What I wasn't mentioning is that I had no doubt because I had not only looked her up myself, but Bea had told stories about Honey over the years, her voice always filled with the type of pride I had only before heard come from a parent. Bea might not have had any biological kids, but Honey was as close in her mind as one could be and that much was clear.

"And," Alonso added, voice slipping into a tone

that had my hackles all the way raised. "She said *you* think she's cute. She said you said she was, and quote me here, 'hot as fuck'."

My jaw dropped as I tried to find the words to say. It took me a few moments before they came to me, but all I could do was deny. "Cady is a lying liar who lies."

"Cady said you would say that." He laughed into the receiver when he heard my affronted groan. "Are you sweet on her, Mimi? Is she everything you dreamed of and more?"

I groaned again. "Please shut up."

"Uh oh. Did I hit a nerve little sister?" He asked.

"Go all the way to hell."

"Ah," he crooned. "A nerve it is."

"You're ridiculous."

"Mhm. That fact has been well documented," he replied. "But what I find utterly fascinating is how you're avoiding the question."

I sighed as I finished my counts and closed the drawer. I knew he wasn't going to just let this go and hanging up on him now was a good way to find myself subjected to the conversation again in the near future, otherwise known as him calling me every hour on the hour until I get annoyed enough to answer the phone. "Fine. Yes, Honey is objectively attractive. But that doesn't matter because she's not my type."

"Which means she is *exactly* your type."

My face went hot, and I sputtered out a response as he cackled in my ear. "I'm done with this. Goodbye."

"No, wait. I'm sorry, okay? I just think it's high time for you to put yourself out there."

"And I just think it's time for you to mind your business," I retorted. "Things are complicated enough without me making them even more complicated. Just let it go."

There was a muffled noise on his end, and someone called his name, and I heard him sigh. "Fine," he said, finally relenting. "You're lucky I need to go anyway, but don't think we're done with this conversation. I'm onto you."

I snorted. "Sure, if you say so."

His chuckle had me smiling. I never could stay mad at him. "And I mean it. You know we all love you and love Bea. We just miss you and want you to be happy."

The words pressed something warm and painful into my chest, and I had to swallow hard against the sudden lump in my throat and the fresh burn of tears in my eyes.

"I love you all too," I whispered. "I'm okay, Alonso. Really. Please let mom and dad know that too. I know they worry, but I promise I'm where I want to be."

"I will," he agreed. "But also, don't block your blessings especially when they're in the form of a leggy woman who looks really good even in a shitty black and white photo."

I groaned. "Hang up."

"I'm hanging, I'm hanging. Night sis."

"Night."

I disconnected the call and silence settled back over the bakery, thick and familiar. It didn't take long for me to finish closing up and click the lights off plunging the place in relative darkness. I moved through the final few parts of my closing routine on instinct before finally walking out the door and locking it behind me. When I stepped outside, the late summer air blew strong enough to tickle the back of my neck and I shivered. There were still a few people walking along the sidewalks on their way to the diner or just enjoying the evening. It was still warm in the way that Georgia was on a late summer night, but I found it enjoyable. Sometimes I wished I could walk from the town back home, but it was still too warm for that, and I wasn't trying to walk on the side of the road at night.

When I pulled up the driveway, the lights were on and for a moment I was confused until I saw Honey's car. I sighed when I pulled up to park beside it and took a moment to lean my head back against the seat. Today was harder than usual and I wasn't sure if I was ready to deal with someone who seemed to think my presence was an attack. Especially not when I was still dealing with everything else. For a moment, I thought about calling Cassandra and asking to crash at her place for the night. But then again, she would probably want to talk about Honey too and I'd never hear the end of it. It was better to just face things and get it over with. I could keep this all strictly business.

But as I walked up the stairs to the house, the truth throbbed quietly under my ribs, traitorous and warm. Honey Parker was already under my skin and some small, reckless part of me wasn't sure I minded.

Chapter 7

Honey

My hand shook slightly as I shut and locked the front door behind me. I leaned back against it and took a deep breath in, trying to steady myself. Bea's house settled around me in that way old houses did with the gentle creaks of wood sounding like the heavy exhales of memories. Late afternoon sunlight spilled through the foyer in slanted bars, bathing the floor in deep oranges and reds. The house was too damn quiet. It was the kind of quiet that made my thoughts that much louder.

I pressed the heels of my hands to my eyes, but it did nothing to curb my swirling thoughts as I turned over the attorney's words again and again in my mind. Bea had mingled my inheritance with Mimi in a way that meant long conversations and maybe even more lawyers getting involved.

Inheritance from the family you never knew.

If guilt had a sound, it would've been this voice inside me that was slowly but surely becoming more impossible to ignore.

Maybe Bea should have left it all to her.

I set my purse on the hall table, but my fingers lingered on the strap like I wasn't ready to let go. My throat was tight, and my lungs felt too small for the air inside them. There was this awful sense of something slipping through my grasp; something I never even got to touch properly before losing it.

Bea—the aunt I barely knew. A family I could have had if I had just reached out and tried to bridge that gap. There were so many questions I had kept to myself over the years—questions that I just assumed I would one day be able to ask. I would never get those answers now.

My eyes stung at the realization that I had taken so much for granted. I had let myself get so caught up in the immediacy of life that I never really stopped to think 'what if'. I blinked hard, forcing myself to breathe slowly. I'd spent years perfecting the art of staying composed. When you grew up with a father who hated questions and a stepmother who preferred everything easy and uncomplicated, you learned quickly that emotions should be tidied and tucked away like clutter. But here, in Bea's house, surrounded by the ghost of her life and the memories of a family I didn't get to know, all my practiced neatness was falling apart at the seams.

I moved automatically, walking into the kitchen and trying to find something else to focus on. I opened a cabinet, barely peeking inside before I closed it again. When I opened the drawer in front of me, there was a stack of recipe cards, the words written in that familiar looping scrawl. I ran a fingertip over the paper imagining I could hear Bea and the way she would talk to herself as she cooked. It was such a random memory and yet one that wasn't touched by the passage of time. I swallowed hard and closed the drawer before passing my fingertips over the familiar tea kettle like it was my anchor to this new reality.

The worst part was how little I knew. Not just about Bea but about myself too. I didn't know what to do with all of this. What would the family have wanted? Hell, what would Bea have wanted? I thought back to the one time I'd tried to ask my dad about Bea and my family and even my mom. I must've been thirteen or fourteen. I was naïve enough to think that maybe he had been saving these conversations for when I was older, and I had decided I was old enough to handle whatever he told me.

"Dad, I just want to know about mom and her family. I just want to get to know her."

He hadn't shouted. He never had to. His silence felt like a slammed door all on its own. He'd closed the file he was reading with this controlled precision, set his pen down, and said he had to get to the office early. That was it. There was no explanation, and no room for me to ask anything more. He'd walked past me, not sparing me an extra glance and I'd stood there frozen at his very obvious dismissal of my words. It hadn't been until I heard the garage door open and his car start that I'd thought to go after him. By then it had been too late and he was gone.

Later that evening, Melanie had found me at the kitchen counter, pretending to not be upset and failing miserably.

"Honey," she'd said, smoothing her perfectly-mani-cured nails over my shoulder. "You shouldn't upset your father like that. Dwelling on the past isn't helpful. Focus on the future instead."

Focus on the future. Focus on being agreeable. Focus on being easy to handle. Focus on being easy to love.

She'd left me in the kitchen then, tears streaming down my face until the salt burned against my skin. That was the first and last day my father had ever made me cry. It was also the last time I ever asked him about my mother. I focused on school and securing a future where I wasn't reliant on someone else to provide for me, and the past slipped away, kept behind lock and key in the back of my mind.

Now it was here again, unavoidable and sharp-edged, and I couldn't help feeling like I'd failed someone I never got to know. In Bea's letter, she'd said she was as much to blame as my father, but the real enemy here was me.

The air felt heavy, pressing down on me. I sank into the same kitchen chair as earlier, ignoring my closed laptop in favor of resting my forehead against my clasped hands. A tear slipped loose, making its way down my cheek before I swiped it away angrily. Crying wouldn't fix anything. It wouldn't bring Bea back. It wouldn't give me another chance to ask any of the questions I kept inside out of fear of disappointing the people raising me. My phone rang, startling me. I wanted to ignore it, but with a sigh, I stood and walked back to the foyer to grab it from my purse. I was relieved to see Terri's, my best friend from back home, name on the screen. I took a deep breath, wiped my face, and answered.

"Girl," she said in lieu of hello, launching into conversation the way she always did. "How's Hickory Hills?"

"Hickory Springs," I corrected automatically.

"Whatever. How's the pilgrimage back to the place of your birth? Did you find out you're secretly a princess? Are the locals as weirdly nice as we thought they'd be?"

I huffed out a laugh that sounded less amused and more like I was in pain. "I don't know if 'weird' is the word I'd use now, but everyone has been nice, yes."

She went quiet for half a beat, long enough to shift her whole vibe from joking to entirely too perceptive. "What happened?"

Everything. Nothing. Too much and not enough.

"Nothing. It's just...I had to go see the attorney," I said, picking at a chipped bit of polish on my thumbnail. "And I found out all these things about Bea and the land and...I don't know, Terri. I feel like I wasn't made for any of this."

"Of course you were made for it." She replied. "It's your birthplace. That's literally how that works."

"Is it?" I whispered. "Because I don't feel like I fit in here."

"That's how it is when you return to a place you haven't visited in years." Her voice softened in that rare way she only used when she was worried. "That's what finding yourself is all about. Complicated feelings and being messy as hell until you figure things out. Embrace the journey. Just because you feel like a stranger now, doesn't mean the connection isn't real."

Her words hit something deep and raw inside my chest.

"And your dad and Melanie?" she asked, like she already knew the answer. "Are they giving you a hard time about all this?"

I hesitated. "Not exactly," I replied.

"Honey," she said, her voice dropping low and sounding just as frustrated as it always did when my father was brought up in conversation. "That's not a no."

I rubbed my forehead. "He's just impatient. He wants me to go ahead and sell the farm and come back to Chicago."

"Of course he does. Anything to get you back under his thumb and away from having a thought of your own." She paused. "You're not actually considering selling your family's land, are you?"

"I don't know," I admitted. "It's...a lot."

"Yeah, well, so is life. And with the price of land right now? Girl, you'd be out of your mind to let that place go before understanding what it is and what it could be."

I swallowed. The truth in her voice stung even worse because I knew she was right.

"And what about work?" she pressed. "Marisol still being an absolute—"

"Yes." I cut in before she could finish. "She's her usual self."

"When," Terri demanded, "are you going to leave

that place before you work yourself into a damn heart attack?"

"Terri—"

"No, seriously. That woman has nearly driven me to drink, and I don't even work for her. She sets unreasonable expectations that anyone would balk at, but then you manage to outperform and instead of being grateful, she does it again."

Before I could defend myself, the front door opened. I glanced over in time to see the handle turn and watch Mimi appear. She looked up in surprise at seeing me standing in the foyer. Her expression was unreadable, but there was something familiar behind her dark brown eyes. She looked...tired. I could relate.

"Evening," she said gently. "Have you eaten yet?"

The question was simple. The concern behind it wasn't.

I straightened and shrugged. "No, not yet. I'm not really hungry though."

She nodded like she understood all the words I wasn't saying. "Okay. I'm not either. I'll just heat up some leftovers after I shower and then if you get hungry later, you're more than welcome to them."

She gave me a small, polite smile that I recognized immediately as one of those almost-smiles held together by sheer willpower and the desire to not break down in front of someone. It felt strange to see a part of myself echoed in someone and reflected back to me. I wanted to reach out and tell her I got it, but before I could say anything else, she slipped upstairs without another word.

As soon as her footsteps faded, Terri whistled low through the phone. "Now who was that because they sounded hot as fuck."

I felt my cheeks heat at her description. Not because she was wrong, but because secretly I agreed that Mimi had a nice voice. Hell, she had a lot of nice things, not that she needed me to tell her that. "My... housemate," I muttered.

Her tone perked all the way up. "Oh? Do elaborate."

"You're impossible."

"And you're avoiding the question," she pointed out.

"You didn't ask a question; you made a demand." When she said my name in that tone I knew too well, I pinched the bridge of my nose not wanting to deal with any of this but knowing I was going to have to. "Her name is Mimi. She's part of all this stuff with the land and Bea's will. But it's not like that. Things are just..."

"Complicated," she finished for me. Right then, the sharp wail of a crying child erupted in the background and Terri groaned.

"Oh, for the love of—Honey, I have to go. My tiny

demon is summoning me." There was more rustling before another cry echoed over the line. "But listen. Be gentle with yourself, okay? Give yourself time to figure all this out. This might be the only chance you get to try to find what you've been missing."

"Okay," I whispered, nodding though I knew she couldn't see me. When I hung up the phone, I felt a little lighter than before. The conversation didn't solve my problems, but it gave me a small place to start. Maybe I was being too defeatist. I had really only been here one day. That wasn't enough time to figure anything out.

I walked into the living room and looked around. Bea's house creaked softly around me; its old, tired wooden bones settling for the night. It was still strange being inside a place that belonged to someone I had a connection to but barely knew. Someone whose name sat at the corner of my present and a future I couldn't yet see.

And then what about Mimi? How did she fit into everything? How was I supposed to handle figuring out how to split everything up so I could go back to the life I had grown wearily accustomed to. Did I even want to?

Sell the farm. Come home. Don't drag this out.

That's what my father had said when I told him what was going on. He didn't say 'don't disappoint me', but he didn't have to. I could hear it in every word he spoke. I always could.

"Get it together, Honey," I whispered, bracing myself on the counter.

My reflection stared back at me from the window with tired eyes. Somehow, my hair had started coming loose from the bun I'd twisted it into that morning, and my mascara was faintly smudged like dark shadows beneath each eye. I looked like someone who'd been trying too hard for too long to pretend that everything was fine. For whatever reason, I didn't want Mimi to see this version of me. I didn't understand why I cared. Maybe it was because she was now my only living connection to my family. And wasn't that just a kick in the ass. I had to go to someone else to find a connection to my blood relations. It had my chest tightening again with guilt. I needed something to do to take my mind off things.

I pulled the fridge open, searching for the leftovers Mimi had mentioned. Maybe it was rude, but I decided to heat them up myself. So far, Mimi had been nothing but welcoming and I had been nothing but standoffish and cold. Yes, part of that was because she was a stranger, but I was starting to realize that part of it was jealousy. I was jealous that she had enjoyed a relationship with Bea in my stead. I was jealous that she got to know the aunt I would never truly know.

I thought about sweeping my hand in and knocking everything to the ground. Mimi had cooked this food with quiet care and steady hands, and yet here I was wanting to toss it down like a petulant child who didn't get her way. The thought hit me deeper than it should have.

I grabbed the pasta dish and set it on the counter, pulling down two bowls even though she'd mentioned heating the food up herself. I could at least pretend I was being thoughtful instead of an emotional black hole. I portioned out the food and popped it into the microwave before resting my forehead against the cabinet door.

Terri's voice echoed faintly in my head.

Give yourself time to figure all this out. This might be the only chance you get to try to find what you've been missing.

I knew she was right and that terrified me. If she was, that meant I was going to be here longer than I thought. Every time I thought about Bea, I thought about the version of myself that might've existed if I'd really truly known her. Who would I be if my father hadn't shut every door to the past in my face? How different would life be if Melanie hadn't insisted that asking questions and upsetting him meant ruining the future we were supposed to focus on?

What would life be like if I hadn't listened?

Would I have answers if I had pushed just a little bit harder?

The microwave beeped, pulling me back into my body and out of my circling thoughts. I took the bowls out carefully and set them on the table before grabbing two forks. The house felt too full of everything I didn't know and everything I couldn't ask anymore.

Deciding on a plan of action, I padded down the hallway toward the stairs. "Dinner's ready if you want to join me," I called out.

My voice echoed up the dim stairwell, slipping into the shadows where I knew Mimi had retreated. I expected her to ignore me—God knew I wouldn't have blamed her—but after a moment, I heard a door open and soft footsteps making their way toward the stairs.

I straightened instinctively when she appeared, nerves fluttering at the sight of her. I told myself it was just because of the questions I needed to ask and not because she looked beautiful with shadows skirting across her skin.

"Thanks," she murmured when she reached the bottom step, her voice warm despite the weariness.

I nodded, suddenly aware of how awkward I probably looked just standing there, shuffling my feet like a toddler needing to pee. When she smiled, the knot in my chest loosened half an inch. I walked back into the kitchen acutely aware of her following close behind me. I gestured at the dining table before sitting. We were both quiet as we began eating. I wasn't sure how exactly to bring it up, but the question of Mimi and Bea's relationship had been on my mind since speaking with Russell and not having answers was going to wreck my ability to focus on anything else.

"Can I ask you something? Were you and Bea..." I trailed off and gave Mimi a look. "You know...in a relationship?" She frowned for a moment before her eyes widened.

"Oh! No, not even a little bit," she replied, shaking her head frantically. "Bea was straight as a wooden ruler though she was a big-time ally. She and the mailman were fucking last she told me." When she froze as if realizing what she said, her expression was so comical I couldn't help but snort with amusement.

"That's what the attorney said too, though not in those exact words."

Mimi chuckled though it sounded more guilty than amused. "Sorry, that was crass of me to just blurt it out like that, but that's how she described it to me when I caught them once." She shook her head as a fond smile etched itself on her face. "Henry is his name. I know he was wild about her. She talked about him proposing but she was steadfast about not wanting to get married."

Her answer shouldn't have relieved me as much as

it did, but I couldn't help it. That part of me that liked the way Mimi sounded when she laughed was glad to know I wasn't in an episode of Sweet Home Alabama or Kentucky Cousins.

"Wow, I never knew," I replied before taking a bite of pasta. I chewed thoughtfully as I tried to remember what few memories I had. "She never mentioned him to me I don't think."

Mimi nodded. "She probably wouldn't have. She didn't really mention him to me either, at least not until they got caught." She snorted and shook her head. "Then again, she didn't really talk about him after they got caught either."

I nodded, letting the information marinate for a moment. I knew Bea had never had children, but that was the extent of it. My cell beeped, startling me and I sighed when I saw Marisol's name on the screen. When I looked back up, Mimi was staring at me with a peculiar expression.

"What is it?" I asked.

She frowned for a moment, before shaking her head. "Nothing."

I was tempted to let that go, but I figured if I wanted to ease into questions, I probably needed to start somewhere. "I can tell you wanted to say something. It's alright. You can ask me whatever. Doesn't mean I'll answer, but you can ask."

Mimi looked at me for a moment before speaking. "You just looked so annoyed when the person texted you, so I wondered if everything was okay."

I swallowed hard at that. "Oh. Yeah, it's just my boss asking for something. No big deal." That was definitely a lie. Whatever she wanted and whenever she wanted it was always a big deal let her tell it. Still, it had been a long day, and I wasn't in the mood to deal with her requests right now. I needed a stress-free night to plan how I was going to attack all of my other issues.

"It's kind of late for all that isn't it?"

I wish. I nodded but then shrugged when I really thought about it. Marisol never really kept to strict business hours even when I first started. I had grown so accustomed to answering that I really didn't pay much attention to the time these days when she reached out. Most of my meals were eaten while still working as it was. I didn't have anyone at home to eat with, so I was usually free to create my own schedule.

"Sorry if that's prying," Mimi said quickly when I didn't respond right away. I shook my head.

"It's totally alright. You're not wrong anyway," I confirmed. "But if you don't mind, I have a few questions about Bea I'd love for you to answer if you're not busy tonight?"

Mimi nodded. "Ask away. I'll tell you whatever you want to know."

Chapter 8

Mimi

I stood at the edge of the eastern apiary, the early afternoon light draping itself over the rows of white-painted hive boxes like a soft shawl. The bees were active today—no doubt thanks to the warm summer air that kept them energized and buzzing this way and that as they searched for flowers and food for the hive. The sunlight had me sweating inside my suit, but I couldn't deny the day was quite picturesque with perfectly blue skies and the grass vibrantly green as it swayed in the soft breeze. I hovered close to the hive, my gloved hands resting lightly on my hips as I listened to the familiar hum that usually settled my nerves.

It wasn't quite doing it for me today unfortunately.

My thoughts kept drifting back toward the kitchen at Bea's house and the quiet morning routine Honey and I had somehow fallen into without even talking about it. It had only been three days since she first stepped foot into my life, all city polish layered over quiet grief in a combination I still hadn't completely figured out. And yet, in the middle of all that uncertainty, we'd created a rhythm.

I'd pad into the kitchen just after sunrise to make my tea, and Honey would already be at the table with her laptop open and hair pulled back in that signature bun that left me with a clear view of her neck. I knew I shouldn't imagine how that honeyed skin would feel with my lips against it, but it was damn near impossible to keep my mind from wandering. She always looked like she wasn't fully convinced smiling before nine in the morning was allowed. But she'd do it anyway, offering me a soft 'good morning' that hit me dead in the chest in a way I really and truly tried to ignore. More often than not, I had to pause and collect myself, staring out the kitchen window as I remembered she was probably grieving and not looking to be fawned over by my goofy ass. It was becoming a problem or at least a puzzle. A gorgeously confusing puzzle.

We hadn't talked about the land or how we might divide the acreage. We hadn't talked about finances or what Honey wanted to do with the house. I wasn't sure if she was avoiding the topic or simply too overwhelmed to start, and I didn't want to push.

I leaned closer to one of the hive entrances,

watching a worker bee fan her wings to cool the brood inside. "I wish I knew what you all were thinking," I murmured. "It'd make life a whole lot easier if I had hundreds of other opinions to poll."

"Talking to the bees again?"

I turned to see Cassandra approaching. Her veil was pushed back, and her forehead was dotted with sweat thanks to the late summer sun. She carried her smoker loosely in one hand, looking annoyingly amused for someone who'd spent her whole morning elbow-deep in hive inspections.

"Always," I said, tugging off my gloves. "They're better listeners than most people."

"Oh, I don't know about that," Cassandra said, raising a teasing brow. "Depends on the people. Speaking of people, how are things going with Honey? Is she as sweet as her name suggests?"

I tried not to react, but when Cassandra's grin spread like wildfire, I knew I wasn't the least bit successful. It's not like I didn't want to talk to her about Honey. Hell, I needed all the help I could get when figuring out how to broach the uncomfortable conversations I knew we needed to have. Falling off my horse and nearly breaking my damn back was easier to deal with than having to look into Honey's eyes and ask her what she planned on doing with Bea's inheritance.

"It's going fine," I said, which was mostly true if I

ignored everything else. "Better than I expected. She seems to be adjusting well to everything though she mostly just seems to work, eat and sleep."

Cassandra laughed low, like she knew every secret I hadn't told her. "Are you saying that the girl is boring?"

"No," I said. "It's just that Bea talked about her all the time, but not in ways that prepared me for any of this."

"And the legal stuff?" she asked, leaning against a hive stand. "Has she talked to Russell about the land?"

"She did. He called to let me know. But I still can't get a read on what she wants to do about everything, and I don't want to push her before she's ready." I glanced away taking in the fields as I tried to think about how I would feel if I were in her position. "I know she and Bea were estranged, but even now when she talks about Bea...it feels like I'm missing something and I just don't want to overstep."

"I mean, I feel like that's reasonable," Cassandra said. "Though the gossip train is saying she was supposedly spotted talking to one of those development guys who's been sniffing around town. Tasha said one of those guys came into the market asking too many questions and not buying a damn thing."

My head snapped up. "What? When was this?"

"Maybe a couple days ago." Cassandra looked up

with a hum. "I know you said she had gone to town and talked to Russell, so I thought maybe they were confused about that, but the ladies at bingo were adamant that someone saw her chatting with a guy who was most definitely not him."

"But that's a big leap to go from her talking to some random person to her talking to a developer about selling the land."

Cassandra held up both hands. "Hey, don't bite my damn head off. I didn't say I believed it, I'm just telling you what's going around in case you weren't aware of what was being said. Even if she was talking to the guy, she might not actually know who he is or what's been going on around here given she's not lived in town for years."

"But still, why would they—?" I stopped myself. Speculating on things instead of just asking outright was not helpful and would only lead to misunderstandings and hurt feelings. "I'll talk to her tonight. I need to anyway since we're supposed to start going through Bea's things and seeing what..." I trailed off, not ready to finish that sentence. I should be ready for this. It had been a month, and I knew from conversations with Bea exactly what she wanted me to do with most things. She would have kicked my butt to see me holding on to her stuff like I was.

Cassandra's teasing dropped away immediately. "Are you sure you're ready for that?"

"No," I said before exhaling slowly. "But I'm not the only one who matters here and I think delaying the inevitable will just make it even harder later on down the road. Plus, I still don't know how long Honey plans to be here. There are just too many unknowns right now and something has to give."

Cassandra stepped forward and squeezed my shoulder. "You're doing right by her. I think Bea would be really proud."

I hoped so. I desperately hoped so.

By the time dinner rolled around, I'd spent more time rehearsing how to bring up us sorting through Bea's things than I'd spent actually cooking the chicken and vegetables on my plate. Honey sat across from me at the small kitchen table, poking halfheartedly at her food, her thoughts clearly somewhere else. Things were tense in a way they haven't been since that first day she came. It seemed so strange to think that she had almost been here for a week and yet we were no closer to sorting things out than we were before she came. I waited until we were mostly done before broaching the subject that had been on my mind all afternoon.

"So," I began gently. "I wanted to ask if you think you're up for going through Bea's room. Her things, I mean. She kind of left it up to us in her will though she did talk a little before…before she left about what she hoped would happen to certain things."

Honey froze for a moment before she set her fork back onto her plate.

When she looked at me, her gaze was steady though I could see something swirling just behind her eyes. "Why haven't you gone through them yet?" Her words sounded accusatory though I could hear the genuine curiosity in her tone. Even still, there was a fragileness in the way she framed the question.

I swallowed hard, tightening my grip on my napkin. "Well, I knew Bea would want you here first, and I didn't want to touch or move anything without your consent. She was your family."

Honey pressed her lips together before looking away. She was silent for a moment, but I could see her throat bobbing as she swallowed. When she finally looked back at me, her eyes were suspiciously shiny, but I tried not to draw attention to it. I felt the telltale burn of unshed tears myself when I thought about finally opening the door to Bea's room. It wouldn't be the first time I'd gone in there since her death, but it would be the first time I went in with a purpose.

"I suppose I also didn't want to start going through her things because then it would make this all real." I hadn't meant to be so vulnerable, but I couldn't find it in me to regret my words; not when Honey looked at me like she understood and maybe even felt the same.

"Thank you," she whispered. "I really appreciate that actually. I didn't really think about the fact that Bea would have things that needed to be sorted through or that I would be the one doing it. But I'm glad I'm not doing it alone. I think that would have been even worse."

I nodded, trying to keep my own emotions from spilling over. "Whenever you're ready," I said softly. "We can go as fast or as slow as you need." I meant it. Even if waiting felt like being stretched thin, I meant every word.

"And you as well," Honey replied firmly. "You were here with Bea for so long, and I can tell you really loved her, so...same."

I blinked quickly, trying desperately to keep the tears at bay. "Thanks, Honey."

We finished our food and then washed dishes in quiet coordination—Honey washing and me, rinsing and stacking them to air-dry. We barely exchanged more than a few soft 'thank you's' even when our fingers slipped over one another's every so often. It was familiar in a strange, comforting sort of way. I wondered if Bea were still here, and Honey came to visit, would our evenings have been like this? Would Bea have sat back and let Honey and I stand shoulder to shoulder at the sink, or would she have taken charge? Would she tease me about my obvious attraction to her niece, or would she warn me to stand clear of her? I had so many questions and yet the answers stayed frustratingly blank.

When we finished, I wiped my hands on the hand towel and tried to calm the furious thump of my heart. "We don't have to go through everything tonight," I said gently. "But if you're sure you're ready for this, we can at least start."

Honey hesitated, her gaze flicking down the hallway as if Bea's bedroom door were the edge of a cliff. For a moment I was sure she would step back from that precipice and say maybe we could do this tomorrow. But then she breathed deep and looked over at me with a determined expression.

"I'm ready," she whispered. "If anything, we need to at least do an inventory on what's still in there and that way we can come up with a plan of attack."

I nodded in agreement before leading the way down the hallway, the wooden floor creaking under every step. I'd avoided this for weeks. It was easy enough when my bedroom was upstairs. Now, my stomach knotted tighter with each step we took until I was sure it would never untangle.

I opened the door slowly, not sure what I was expecting. Maybe I had hoped that Bea would be there, standing just on the other side with her hands on her hips and a smile on her face. Instead, the air inside smelled stale, waning light from the window bathing the room in mauve and purple while still giving us enough illumination to see. Under the dust, there was an ever-present scent of lavender and chamomile lotion. It felt like she had just stepped out to check the hives and would be back any minute, shaking her head about forgetting her glasses again.

The ache in my chest hit like a damn sledge-hammer and I took in a sharp breath before catching myself. This wasn't the time for me to break apart. We still had so much to do. Before I could say anything, a small sound from behind me pulled my attention. I glanced over my shoulder, eyes widening when I saw Honey standing just inside the doorway with one hand pressed against her mouth as tears, silent and fat slipped down her cheeks. These weren't soft tears. These were the fierce kind that pulled from deep inside before leaving you a hollowed-out husk.

"Honey?" I asked softly, turning completely to face her. "Are you okay?" I knew it was a ridiculous question as soon as it left my lips and that was confirmed when she shook her head.

"No," she whispered, voice breaking. "I can't do this."

"Honey—"

"No," she croaked out. The emotions in her gaze were unmistakable: grief, horror, and a self-loathing so strong I could practically taste its acrid flavor in the back of my throat. This was Honey cracked open and as much as I'd wanted to know her thoughts, I hadn't wanted it to be like this. I hadn't wanted to see her broken and falling apart.

"It isn't fair." Her voice tore apart mid-sentence. "Bea's gone and I never got to apologize. I wasn't here for her. I didn't even know she was sick and I didn't get to come back. I didn't even try, and now I can't say anything. I can't—"

Her knees buckled and I hurried, not making it before she dropped loudly to the floor, sobs ripping free like something long buried had finally forced its way to the surface. I didn't even think before I followed her down, wrapping my arms around her before she could fold in on herself.

She pressed her face into my shoulder, her whole body shaking so hard I felt it in my bones and nearly to my soul. There was no holding this back. This was a wave of grief so all-consuming that to fight it was to choke and drown. No, this was the type of pain that you had to swim through.

"Let it out," I murmured, gently cradling the back of her head and pressing her face further against me as her tears soaked through my shirt. I wrapped my other arm around her waist, holding her like she might sink down to the core of the earth if I didn't anchor her with me on the surface. "Just let it all out and know I'm here to catch you."

My words seemed to open the flood gate and a wail so forlorn it had my skin dimpling and my hair raising ripped itself from her chest. She sobbed into my shirt, her fingers curling around the fabric like she was afraid to let go. I swallowed against my own tears, stroking her hair as the room settled around us.

"It wasn't your fault," I whispered when her sobs finally softened. "You were a kid when whatever it was, happened. I know for a fact Bea didn't hold any of that against you. She never did; not with the way she smiled whenever she said your name."

Honey squeezed her eyes shut, tears still slipping free. "But I did. I held it against myself. I still do and I don't know if I can stop."

My heart cracked wide open at her vulnerability. The strong image she always displayed wasn't a facade, but a shield for someone who felt so deeply it nearly caused her to cave in. I held her tighter, gently rocking her.

"You're here now," I whispered. "And that matters more than you know."

Honey shuddered, a soft, wounded sound falling from her lips as she buried her face against my shoulder again. I could have pushed her to talk, but I knew now what she really needed was someone to be there. Grief and comfort intertwined as our bodies curled together on the floor of Bea's bedroom.

Chapter 9

Honey

I woke to brightness. Not the muted, bluish-gray sliver of dawn that I had become accustomed to leaking through the guest room curtains when I woke up before the sun. No, this was full on rays of light, spearing across my eyelids like someone had turned on a spotlight just to interrogate me. I winced and burrowed deeper into the softness of my pillow enjoying the lavender scent and flannel sheets.

Wait. Flannel sheets?

I opened my eyes then, hissing at the light that stabbed them. Why was everything so warm and why the hell was it so damn bright?

I tried to roll onto my back but found I could barely move because something—or more like *someone's* arm was draped across my waist like the heaviest of blankets. There was also a knee hooked lightly against the back of mine and the steady rise and fall of slow breathing ghosting across the back of my neck, warm and rhythmic. My brain was slow to connect the dots, but when it did, I nearly threw myself from the bed. Instead, I went rigid. Completely statuesque. My heart thudded so hard I could almost hear it echoing in my ears. Carefully I turned my head and peeked over my shoulder, eyes widening when I saw a familiar face.

Mimi.

She was big spooning me and even more, this wasn't my bed—it was *hers*. I wasn't sure exactly what had happened, but I forced myself to catch up, thinking quickly over the past few days and hours.

"Fuck," I whispered trying desperately not to wake her until I was able to reaffix my walls in place. I managed to turn then, slowly and carefully in the circle of her arms until I was on my side staring at her face.

Her features were softer than I'd ever seen them. Coal-dark lashes fanned out against her cheeks and her mouth was parted the tiniest bit as she breathed. The faintest smell of honey lingered around her, warm and sweet, calming me despite the realization that we slept together. This was the first time I had slept in a bed with someone in years and I felt something tight and painful twist under my ribs. I should look away. I should haul myself from beneath these sheets and run so far and fast that I would never be caught again. But my eyes stayed on her, drinking in every detail like I'd been starved for softness and didn't know it until now.

My hand betrayed me before my brain could stop it and I reached up to gently run the pad of my fingers along her cheekbone. Her skin was warm and softer than silk. I drank her in, the morning making me bold in ways I couldn't be normally. Mimi made a small sound and scrunched her nose in a way that hit me low in the stomach and radiated outward like a spark catching dry brush.

No one has the right to be this damn cute in their sleep.

The thought amused me even as I traced her features again, my gaze stopping at her full lips and how utterly kissable they looked. When her arm tensed against my hip, I darted my gaze back up in time to see her eyelids flutter. She blinked at me, slow and unfocused, and then smiled. It was a sleep-soft, crooked little thing that made something in me go molten.

"Good morning," she murmured, voice deep and raspy with sleep. The sound rolled over my skin like velvet, and I fought back a shiver.

"Good morning," I whispered back, acutely aware of every inch where her body touched mine. I could only thank god that we were wearing clothes. I don't know what I would do if I was feeling her bare skin against mine. It had been too long since I'd last been touched and I was too raw to not lean into it and beg for more.

"How are you feeling?" She asked gently. Her arm was still around my waist making the question feel more intimate than she probably meant it to. It took a second to find my words. How could I explain how my mind felt blank and not blank at the same time without sounding completely nonsensical?

"I feel...lighter," I said finally, hoping that that would explain things enough without having to provide too much more. "Which is weird because I think I used up all my water content last night. I should be a raisin." *Great, now I'm rambling.* I hadn't done that in years and it was a true sign that I was not back to my normal compartmentalizing self.

Mimi's laugh was soft and the sound of it skittered down my spine, lighting nerves that I didn't need to feel.

"I understand," she said. "I cried for days in Bea's bed after she passed."

Guilt surged so fast my throat tightened.

"I should've been here," I whispered. "I was thousands of miles away. She was dying and I was working like an asshole and trying to pretend like everything in my life was fine."

Mimi's hand lifted, moving up to rest on my arm.

Her thumb brushed gently across my skin and this time I couldn't hide my shiver.

"Hey," she said, voice firm and tender at once. "You didn't know until the end. Bea wouldn't want you beating yourself up. You're here now, Honey. That's what matters and that's what you should focus on."

Her words slid into me like sunlight into a cold room. I didn't cry. Hell, I was probably dehydrated enough to not have any tears left. Still, something in my chest unknotted just a little. Mimi's arms around me suddenly felt like the safest place in the world. So safe I let myself go not realizing my body's own intent until it was too late and my lips were pressed against hers. The kiss was a little off center, and my lips were definitely chapped and yet I let out a groan that anyone would recognize as pure want. The hand on my arm tightened before pulling me closer and Mimi's lips surged against mine.

Kissing had never been a favorite pastime of mine, but I found myself sinking into this one quickly and with no fuss. Mimi's mouth was made for kissing and when she parted her lips to suck in a breath, I took it as an invitation, dipping my tongue in and tasting the honey from her lips. Mimi's hands pulled me closer and when our breasts pressed together, I didn't know who moaned first. The sound sent such a pulse of pure arousal through me that I had to clench my thighs against the feeling. It was that realization that had me pulling away though as my brain caught up to the fact that I was in Mimi's bed, kissing her like I hadn't just sobbed and admitted that I hated myself for never coming home.

Panic surged through me. I had shown my soft underbelly to someone I barely knew. Not only that, but I didn't regret it. I had wanted Mimi to hear me and understand me. I had wanted to be vulnerable for once and let all of my anger and frustration free instead of letting it choke me into silence and submission. I was here in Mimi's arms and...it felt good.

It felt *too* good.

I pulled away, sitting up awkwardly. The room swayed slightly with the movement, and I had to slam my eyes shut as the décor lurched and my brain caught up with me now being vertical. I could feel the bed shift as Mimi moved. When she let out a small, pained sound, I couldn't stop myself from opening my eyes and looking over at her worriedly.

Mimi shifted again and made another tight little sound.

"Are you okay?"

She gave a half smile. "Yeah. It's just my back being fucking dramatic like it always is in the morning when I wake up."

"Dramatic?"

"Old horse accident," she said, pushing herself into a seated position with careful movements. Then, without hesitation, she stood from the bed and began stretching, lifting her arms overhead until her shirt rode up, exposing her lower torso. She exhaled slowly, arching her back until something popped audibly.

I shouldn't have stared, but there was no way I was going to be able to look away. My lips still tingled, and I knew that the kiss had awakened something that would be difficult to shove back in its cage. The morning light caught on her skin bathing her in warmth. When she bent sideways, slow and controlled, another soft sound escaping her throat, heat flushed up my neck so fast I almost choked on it.

When she looked at me again, I swore she could see exactly where my mind was and it had nothing to do with Bea.

"I should get ready," I blurted out, almost tripping over my own feet as I scrambled off the bed.

"You're more than welcome to take your time or sleep a little more if you need to," she said, amusement warm in her voice.

My breath caught when I thought about lying back down in the bed with her by my side. What if I kissed her again? *What if she kissed me back?* The thought had me nearly sweating, so I did the only thing I could do. I fled. I didn't stop moving until I was in the bathroom with the door locked behind me.

My heartbeat was a frantic drum-line, and my palms were sweating so badly I probably left hand marks on the doorknob. When I looked at myself in the mirror, my eyes were wide and my expression hunted. My lips were puffy, and I nearly touched them to see if they were as sensitive as they still felt. I was so wildly, irrevocably attracted to Mimi it damn near hurt.

"Fuck," I whispered to no one, letting the word fall like my own self-worth.

A shower helped. Sort of. The water was hot, steaming the mirror and filling the bathroom with the clean scent of eucalyptus soap. But the moment I stepped out and made my way to my room, reality slammed back in. I checked the time and saw it was nearly half past ten.

"Work," I breathed. "Shit."

I pulled my hair into a loose ponytail and threw on the first clothes I found. Never had I been late to work outside of something unprecedented happening on the train. Even then, I was usually connected to my phone, answering emails or delegating tasks to make sure everything stayed on schedule. It wasn't that I had never taken a vacation or gotten sick. It's just that it happened so rarely that I didn't even know how to handle this.

I hurried from my room and into the kitchen just in time to see Mimi in her beekeeping suit walking across the backyard. The suit should've looked bulky or awkward, but somehow, she still moved with a natural grace. The morning sun glinted off the white fabric, and she looked like she belonged to the land, and it belonged to her. Something settled painfully in my chest, but I couldn't stop watching even as she disappeared out of view. It was only my phone ringing that finally dragged my gaze away from the window and back to what I was supposed to be doing.

I held up the phone, staring at the screen and wondering what I could do to get out of this conversation with my boss. I wasn't really in the mood for whatever was about to happen, but I still connected the call anyway and decided to just get it over with and move on.

"Honey, where have you been?" she snapped before I even said hello. "Those numbers are late, the client is waiting, and I've had to reschedule two meetings because of you."

"I—"

"This whole trip home has turned into a nightmare. I told you it was bad timing with the Newsome project not shaping up to be finished on schedule or on budget," she continued, not letting me get a word in.

"You should've planned better and delegated if you were just going to slack off when we needed you most."

Heat rose up the back of my neck, and I had to ball a fist to keep from slamming my hand on the kitchen table.

"Marisol, please. If you would just let me ex—"

"You can't just disappear because you're visiting your hometown after a while. People are relying on you. Honestly, Honey, this is unprofessional, even for you—"

Even for me? *Even for me?* Something inside me, something brittle that had been barely holding together with bits of tape and prayers, finally fractured and I found myself speaking before I even realized what I was going to say.

"I apologize, Marisol," I said, my voice shaking with anger. "I'm so incredibly sorry that my family dying has been such an inconvenience for *you*."

Marisol went quiet enough that I could hear a damn pin drop on carpet, but I wasn't done. No. I had years of shit pent up and finally lacked the cap to keep it all bottled inside.

"And if my grief is too disruptive," I continued. "Maybe I should resign so you can find someone more qualified to do the work of three employees."

"Honey, wait. There's no need to be hasty. Let's ta—"

Instead of doing that and listening to her make bullshit excuses that I knew she wouldn't actually mean, I hung up. I was practically vibrating as I opened my laptop, set my 'out of office' message, and logged out of everything. Then I shut it again with a decisive snap. I stood there in the quiet kitchen, my chest heaving and my heart in my damn throat. Terror came first, ice sharp and immediate. What the fuck had I just done? Never had I spoken to anyone like that, especially not my boss.

But beneath it was something lighter and almost exhilarating. I wasn't exactly sure how to describe it, but it felt like I had just chosen myself for the first time in years.

Chapter 10

Mimi

By the time the sun started shifting to the other side of the peach grove, I felt like I'd lived three days inside of one.

Checking the hives that morning had taken longer than usual. The bees were doing well thanks to good temperatures and a lack of bad summer weather. The stores had been steady, and the queens were laying in neat, healthy patterns. Even so, every hive had needed something. A fresh frame here or clearing out burr comb there. It added up, and by the time I finished, my suit smelled like smoke, propolis, and my own stress. That kiss from this morning still lingered in my thoughts and I couldn't help but replay the moment over and over in my mind.

I hadn't known what to expect when I woke up with Honey in my arms. The night had been rough, for both of us. We had spent more than an hour crouched together on the floor in Bea's room before I could coax her to stand and move upstairs. Even then, the way she had clutched at me made it hard to want to put her in her own room and walk away. I had walked us both to my own room with the most innocent of intentions. If I had known what would happen in the morning...I wouldn't have changed a thing. Feeling Honey's lips against mine had me sweating in all the best ways and I'd stood there, shocked and smiling when she'd ran from the room like her ass was on fire.

"Fuck, I am in so much trouble," I had said to any bee that would listen, though none of them had given me any ideas what to do.

From the beehives, I'd headed straight across the property to meet with Carlo, our crop production manager, who was knee-deep in clipboards and weather reports. It was prime picking time, and the grove workers had been running dawn to dusk for the past few weeks. Yields were okay, not great and not terrible, but the long, hot summer had taken its toll. I walked the grove with him, the air thick with the earthy smell of leaf mulch and the slightly bitter scent of broken green husks. The ladder crews were still out among the trees, picking from lush green branches and filling their buckets with quiet determination. After two hours of checking irrigation lines, sorting out work schedules, and pretending I understood half of Carlo's weather-pattern rambling, I drove into town to check on things with Hillary.

The bakery was slower than I expected for a weekday afternoon—just a handful of regulars nursing coffees and trading gossip. The air smelled like cinnamon and brown sugar, warm and thick, and as comforting as an old quilt. I holed up in the back office with the aging desktop computer that made a noise like a dying animal every time I opened QuickBooks. I was halfway through our inventory sheet when the bell chime above the front door rang with a clean, bright *ding* that usually meant someone had made their way inside. But my stomach tensed.

It was stupid, but after that man had come in earlier that week asking questions he had no business asking about selling the bakery, I'd been on edge. Every time that bell chimed, I peeked around the corner. Today, it wasn't him. Just Mrs. Dunlop ordering her usual two blackberry scones, one for now and one for the drive back home. Still, I stayed jumpy.

By the time I finished paperwork, locked up, and drove home, my hair smelled like yeast and powdered sugar, my back ached, and my hands were sticky with honey residue from the honey-drizzled croissants that had become a new crowd favorite since I introduced them a couple weeks ago. But when I pulled up to Bea's house, something felt...different.

The porch light glowed warm against the blue evening sky and fireflies blinking lazily in the yard. The air carried a faint breeze—cooler now, the kind of reminder that hinted that autumn wasn't far away. When I walked through the front door, a fragrance wafted out so delicious it hit me like a slap and made my mouth water. I stopped in the foyer, breathing it in like I'd been underwater all day and that was my first breath of fresh air. That wasn't the smell of leftover takeout. That was real cooking.

I walked into the kitchen, and the warmth hit me first. The whole room smelled like a Sunday supper from my childhood in a way that made my throat tighten. Honey stood at the stove, stirring a pot with focused concentration. She was barefoot and wearing those damn yoga pants that had caught my attention the first day she was here. There was a smear of flour on her forearm and her lips moved like she was muttering instructions to herself.

My heart did an absolutely foolish little flip as I watched her for a moment longer before making my presence known. She turned to look at me and I nearly gasped when her eyes lit up. Was she really happy to see me? The kiss notwithstanding, she had never reacted to me like that before, but I knew I would feel bereft if she never reacted to me like that again. A small, almost shy smile pulled at her mouth.

"Oh," she said. "You're back."

"I am." I stepped inside fully and tried not to shuffle back and forth like a lovestruck teen. "It smells incredible in here."

There was macaroni and cheese in a pan, the cheese still bubbling around the edges. There were also mashed sweet potatoes whipped smooth in Bea's old red ceramic bowl and collard greens steaming in a deep pan. Roast chicken was resting in a roasting pan, steam still rising from it and the fragrant herbs used to season it, drifting in the air. And finally, the cornbread—perfectly golden and shiny with what I hoped was honey butter spread over top of it.

I blinked at it all, overwhelmed in the best of ways.

"What's the occasion?" I asked. "Are you okay?"

Honey's brow crinkled. "What do you mean? Why wouldn't I be okay?"

I set my gloves on the counter, suddenly too aware of the dirt under my nails and the sweat dried at my temples. "Bea used to cook a huge spread like this whenever she was worried or upset. She always said it was her way of quieting her mind and transforming her worries into something delicious and productive."

Honey stilled completely. Shock flickered across her face, and it warmed me to know that I could still see her emotions so clearly on her face. I knew she was probably feeling vulnerable though, so I quickly took back the words.

"Sorry. I didn't mean—"

"No," she cut in gently. Her gaze moved over the dishes. "It's fine. It's actually kind of nice to know that I have something in common with my aunt that connects us. It makes me feel like I'm not totally cut off from the Parker side of my bloodline."

Warmth tugged at my chest.

"If it makes you feel any better, you look a lot like the photos of your mom," I said before I thought better of it.

Her smile thinned. "Yeah. My dad hated that."

"Fuck, I'm sorry," I whispered. "I shouldn't keep bringing up things that hurt. I just—"

"No," she said quickly, shaking her head. "Don't apologize for talking about Bea, ever. I've carried so much guilt for so long that I honestly don't know how I didn't wear grooves into myself with all the back and forth inside my head."

I exhaled slowly. "I can imagine." I glanced up at her and decided to push just a bit more. "I'm more than happy if you ever want to talk to me or even just *at* me about any of this. Sometimes it's easier talking to an outsider about your feelings since they don't have any skin in the game."

For a beat, she didn't say anything, and I let the silence settle over us. I had given her my offer, and I was quickly learning that she often just needed a bit of time to process things before speaking. I thought back to all the things I learned about Honey from Bea's stories. The pride that always colored her words was undeniable even if there was often a thread of sadness in them as well. I knew without a doubt that Bea loved Honey dearly, and she deserved to know that.

"Thank you," Honey said. She looked down at the pot and her expression shifted into something so wistful, I wished I had the power to turn back time. "You're probably right that I need to talk about these things with someone, and you probably knew Bea best toward the end."

When she glanced over at me, I felt something like an electric spark shoot through me. "Also, you're kind of sweaty, so you should probably go shower."

I barked out a laugh not quite expecting that. I looked down and gestured at my dusty jeans and dirt-streaked shirt. "I think I look pretty farm chic, and the 'eau de farmer parfum' sort of gives it a little something."

Her smile then was a little fond and utterly disarming and I felt my heart thump almost audibly.

"I actually don't mind it," she said, eyes glinting

playfully. "But in small doses and definitely not at my kitchen table."

"Oh, is that so?" I teased back, even as my pulse kicked up. "Well, I suppose that since you cooked, I will heed your rules and go make myself more presentable. It'll give me time to decide which side dish I want to find myself in the most when I get back."

My lord. Could I flirt any harder?

"Please do," she said, and I could hear the smile in her voice. "The food and I will be here when you get back."

"That is an offer I would never be able to refuse." Before I could say anything more incriminating, I turned and marched myself down the hallway toward the bathroom. I could still smell the food and my stomach growled loud enough that I heard the faint tinkling of her laughter behind me. I ignored it as I dropped my clothes and stepped into the shower.

Hot water rushed down my back, and I pressed my forehead against the tile as the day washed off me. The scent of orange blossom and honey rose with the steam, familiar and comforting but beneath the warmth of the water and the ache of my muscles, the knowledge that Honey felt more comfortable here tugged at me. I was trying my hardest not to let myself put pressure on how things were progressing, but I knew I was falling. Through all of Bea's stories, I had slowly fallen for the

Honey she'd built up in my mind. Maybe it was my lack of dating over the years or just my inner hopeless romantic inserting herself, but I couldn't help but wonder if Bea was still operating her matchmaking beyond the grave. She had always told me that if I met Honey, I would love her and she wasn't wrong. It might not be love right now, but there was something there. How could I not fall after the spread she made and the way her shoulders had eased when she talked about feeling connected to Bea. I could see love shining from her gaze when she realized they had something in common.

I wanted that gaze on *me*.

I wanted to be the cause of that unguarded, 'sun peeking through the clouds' kind of smile. This feeling was ridiculous, and yet I didn't care. Hickory Springs had become my safe haven and place of healing. Bea's family had become my own and I didn't want to give this up. I loved my family, but this place was my *home*. The kiss between Honey and me had shifted something. She had looked at me like I wasn't just someone sharing a house out of convenience. She looked at me like she trusted me. Like she wanted to trust me even more and I was fucking hooked.

Chapter 11

Honey

Waking up in Hickory Springs was a completely different experience than waking up in downtown Chicago. Outside was peaceful, with a few birds chirping and the brush of the breeze through leaves. Inside, there was always something creaking or humming like the house itself was singing. I asked Mimi once if the house was haunted, but she'd just shook her head and started laughing. When I asked Cassandra the same thing, she jokingly said 'maybe' before wandering off to do whatever it was she did all day. It had been two weeks since I came to town, and I was still trying to get used to being able to hear myself think.

My eyes were gritty, lids sticking faintly as I blinked up at the ceiling. A ray of morning sun slipped between the curtains, warming the air and making me throw off my blankets. My head felt heavy and my throat was raw and scratchy in a way that made me remember too clearly what last night had been: another trip down a memory lane I didn't actually remember. Mimi and I had combed through Bea's room, opening boxes and classifying things we found so we knew what to do with them. It was hard to see the life of someone I would never truly get to know again, but it was also nice to see that there was still so much of me there.

Bea had kept every letter I sent her as a kid, even as they grew shorter and fewer. She had printed off pictures of me and made an entire picture journal showcasing my growth from awkward kid to college student. She even had pictures of me walking across the university stage when I had no idea she'd been there.

"She told me Melanie had let her know and sent her a ticket," Mimi had offered when she saw me freeze at the images. That had been one of the biggest shocks for me given how Melanie hated anytime my mom was brought up. It hadn't made me look at Melanie in a new light, but it did make me curious why.

I'd been fielding calls from her and my father as they tried to understand why I wasn't back yet. Work was usually the excuse I used when I didn't want to talk to them, and they always accepted it. But after the conversation with Marisol, and without letting myself think long enough to talk myself out of it, I'd submitted a request for time off for the next month while I decided on my next move. I'd checked my email and handled the frantic messages from my colleagues, of course. There always were frantic messages honestly, and normally I would give in and handle everything myself. I didn't do that this time. This time, I forwarded everything, routing it to the exact people who could keep the project from imploding without my input.

I had *months* of leave saved. Hell, over the years, I had accrued enough time off to vanish off the grid until the new year. That alone made something deep in my chest twist. What kind of person worked that much without noticing?

Me, apparently.

I shoved the thought away and pushed myself upright. My body felt heavy, as if I'd been dragged along the bottom of a river. I scrubbed my hands over my face and forced myself up. The bathroom was calling and the idea of hot water sliding over my skin felt heavenly after a night full of crying and reminiscing. Plus...the kissing. It was like that one morning had woken up everything in me that screamed out for companionship. Mimi's kisses were like a balm against the burn of my eyes and the grief in my lungs. Her touch seemed to soothe an ache that I had spent years denying even existed.

I didn't understand how I had lived without it until now, but I was tired of denying myself the things I wanted, and she had seemed to be all aboard every time she leaned in and kissed me harder. We hadn't gone farther than kissing though. It was the same with our conversations about the farm. She had brought out the documents showing the formation of the non-profit as well as how the farm's meager profits were spent, but we hadn't sat down and really discussed what to do now. I didn't know the first thing about owning a farm or a bakery for that matter. I couldn't be any less equipped to have my name attached to these deeds even if I tried and yet every time Mimi smiled at me, I found myself holding onto ownership that much tighter. That Denton guy had found me again on one of my random walks around downtown, but I'd given him more vague answers and kept it pushing. I wasn't sure how I felt about him and his habit of popping up randomly. It didn't even seem like he was from here and that gave me pause.

I sighed softly as I thought about all the decisions waiting for me and I knew I couldn't hide out in my room forever. I only had two more weeks of leave from work, and I couldn't leave my job or Mimi hanging. I needed to woman up and make some hard decisions.

I padded down the hallway, my feet cold against the cool hardwood floor. Even with it being hot as hell outside, I was freezing this morning. Mimi said it was probably from the emotional toll. Cassandra said it was because I was cold-blooded as fuck. I liked her answer a lot actually. She was some much-needed comedic relief in the tragedy that was my life as of late. Halfway to the bathroom, the door opened and Mimi stepped out, wrapped in nothing but a towel. I froze as every functioning brain cell evacuated the premises.

The towel was tucked securely under her arms, but her shoulders were bare and glistening, little droplets of water catching the light as they slid over her skin. Her hair was still wet, curling in tight spirals that stopped just above her shoulder. Her thighs peeked out below the towel, and it did nothing to hide the curves on Mimi's frame. When I breathed in to say something and maybe apologize for startling her, my mouth fell open even though no words came out. She smelled like peaches and fucking honey.

Not in an artificial sort of way that often gave me migraines, but in that soft, summer-warm scent that hit just before fruit ripens kind of way. The fragrance was sweet, subtle, and reminded me of sunny days laid out in the grass as I nibbled on peaches and let the juice run down my arm. The memory faded away, and I came back into myself when I realized Mimi was talking.

"...should be more hot water when you get in. I asked Ray to come over and check out that old heater and see if it needs to be replaced." Her voice was rougher than usual and the rasp of it curled down my spine in a way I absolutely did not need it to.

My brain tried to reboot. Failed. I tried again.

"Good morning." It was the only thing I could think to say when she was standing before me, wet and perfect.

Her lips twitched, the corners tilting like she was trying not to laugh at me. Then she slipped past me, the faint brush of her damp skin grazing my upper arm, warm and soft.

"Good morning to you too. The bathroom is all yours. I'm going to get dressed and make some breakfast if you want to come eat."

"I could eat," I blurted out. My cheeks heated as I realized how that sounded.

Mimi chuckled before walking into her bedroom and shutting the door behind her. I didn't breathe until I heard the door click and then it came out of me in a rush. I stumbled inside the bathroom like someone had unplugged me from reality. After I shut the door, I leaned back against it and let my head thunk against the wood before dropping my face into my hands

"Oh my god," I whispered. How am I even a real adult? I had been so obviously ogling Mimi that there was no way she wouldn't know. Then again, kissing her was probably the first clue, so who was I really trying to fool and why?

I shook my head and pushed off the door. "Shower first, then I can figure out what the hell my life has become."

I let myself enjoy the heat as water slid over my frame, but even then, all I could picture was the curve of Mimi's shoulder and the glint of water sliding over her collarbone. I wanted to follow that droplet with my fingers, or better yet, my tongue. I wanted to know if she tasted as sugar sweet as she smelled. My hands drifted over my own chest, and I hissed softly when my fingertips tripped over my hard nipples. I hadn't even been getting off on my own and I was starting to reach that edge where I usually went out and found a bed partner for the evening. But in a town this small, I wasn't trying to start a scandal. And the only one I even wanted was right down the hall. It wasn't that I thought Mimi wouldn't be amenable, but I was terrified of crossing that line and then never being able to recover. There was so much wrapped up in our relationship that I didn't know what I'd do if it imploded.

I leaned forward, propping myself up with one hand on the wall while the other stole down my belly and between my thighs. My pussy was hot and already slick with my own thoughts. I bit my lips as I pressed further, sliding between my lips and sinking one finger into my own cunt. It wasn't near enough, but when I circled my clit with my thumb, I knew it would at least be enough to get me off. Maybe once I came, I could think straight enough to bring up some difficult conversations.

The running water masked the slick sounds of my own movements as I thrust one then two fingers into my hole and kept circling my clit. Sparks of pleasure had me shifting slightly as I did my best not to fall. All I needed was to go down hard and have Mimi rush in to see me knuckles deep in my own pussy. My body seemed to like that idea though with the way it tightened. I had to swallow hard as my orgasm washed over me just to keep quiet. When the feeling slowly faded away, I felt loose-limbed and a little clearer in the head. Maybe an orgasm every morning was just what the doctor ordered.

After a few deep breaths and mentally telling myself to get a damn grip, I managed to finish showering and pull myself together enough to be presentable. Or at least be capable of walking into a kitchen without tripping over my own tongue.

"I'd much rather trip over Mimi's tongue," I muttered under my breath as I made my way back down the hallway. The scent of eggs and bacon pulling me forward like a neon sign. When I walked in, Mimi was standing at the counter, a steaming mug of what was no doubt tea in her hand as she gazed out the kitchen window. Sunlight streamed over her, setting her skin alight and giving her an ethereal presence. Her hair was surprisingly pulled back in a bun instead of large and free like she normally kept it.

"Good morning again," I said as I came into view.

Mimi turned, her lips immediately shifting into a wide smile and making my chest warm. "Hey you. Are you hungry?"

"Famished," I replied, snickering internally at myself. Her smile didn't change but there was something there just beyond the surface. Or maybe it was just me and my still orgasm-drunk brain trying to see something that didn't exist. I moved to the stove.

"Wait."

I froze at Mimi's word and looked over at her. She gazed at me for a moment before seeming to come to some decision. She set her mug down and walked over to me. When she got close enough for me to be wrapped in her soft fragrance, she reached out brushing her fingers over my cheek before they wrapped around the shell of my ear. I shivered, my gaze trained on her and unable to look away. Her eyes were a dark brown and so inviting that I wanted to sink into them and her lips were full and shiny drawing my attention. She smiled again but didn't step away.

"You had some hair that fell out of your ponytail," she said, answering my unspoken question. That didn't explain why her hand was still there though, shifting to cup my cheek. "But that was really just an excuse to touch you."

"You don't need an excuse," I croaked out, mouth dry.

Her smile was wide and just wicked enough to have my stomach clenching. "True but just touching you would be rude." When she stepped back and dropped her arm, I only had a moment to act, and I didn't want to miss my shot.

I reached out, wrapping my hand around her wrist and pulling her to me. She went with a soft huff of laughter, not fighting me. I leaned in before I could second guess things, brushing my lips over hers. Like always, her lips parted and I darted forward enjoying that flavor I had grown to covet. Her tongue moved with mine even as deceptively strong hands gripped my hips. Kissing her was stronger than a cup of coffee, energizing in all the best ways with none of the fallout. I cupped her cheeks in my hands, diving in with not a care for how hungry or desperate I seemed. Mimi's lips were the perfect taste of heaven.

"Jesus you two. There are four rooms in the house, but you decide to practically fornicate in the damn kitchen."

I groaned at hearing Cassandra's voice before reluctantly breaking the kiss. Mimi's gaze was hazy, and her lips were puffy with the force of our kisses. When her tongue darted out, I almost leaned again. Only the knowledge that Cassandra was probably here for a reason kept me from falling back into Mimi's touch. With a sigh, I stepped back and let my hands fall away.

"You have the worst fucking timing, Cass," Mimi huffed out as she stepped back over to the counter to grab her mug.

I turned and said a guilty 'hello' to Cassandra before loading up my plate with breakfast and going to sit at the table. Mimi and Cassandra seemed to be having some sort of telepathic conversation, but I left them to it as I dug in. I was quickly coming to enjoy southern style breakfasts, especially when it was Mimi making them. Eventually, they finished whatever was going on and joined me at the table.

"You made all this?" Cassandra asked me.

I shook my head and pointed at Mimi. "It was all

her. I'm just here to eat and then figure out what to do for the day."

"What do you mean?" Mimi asked as she piled eggs on her slice of toast. When she glanced up at me, I realized that I hadn't told her what happened.

"Well, I mean...I took leave from my job, so I have just been sort of hanging out here and going through Bea's things." I didn't know what I was expecting, but when her expression softened and her smile looked proud, I almost found myself in tears.

"Good for you. I remember you telling me a little about your boss. You probably deserve to take time off for the next few years with how hard you work."

The warmth that sparked in my chest had my throat tightening unexpectedly and when I looked over at Cassandra, she was smiling my way knowingly. I didn't doubt that she'd realized how I felt about Mimi. She never said anything beyond some harmless jokes, but I wasn't exactly keeping a low profile.

"I don't really know how to not work," I admitted, voice quieter than I meant it to be. "But it feels nice to not be on call all the time."

"You'll figure it out." Cassandra replied before biting into a bacon strip. She chewed thoughtfully before pointing it at me. "If you want something to do, you're more than welcome to join me while I check on our eastern and southern hives."

I grimaced at that. "Um, no thanks. I think bees are great, but I'm still terrified of being stung so I'll let you professionals handle that."

Mimi chuckled. "Well, you can come see the bakery you technically co-own if you want to do that instead. There's honey involved but no bees."

I giggled, the sound a little strange to my ears. I didn't think I had ever laughed as much as I had since coming here. "I don't know..."

"Come on," she nudged, smiling. "It'll give you something to do with your hands besides stress-cooking. Plus, you'll get to meet some of the regulars. I know they have been waiting eagerly to talk to you."

I rolled my eyes, but a tiny smile pushed through. "Fine. But if I burn something, it's totally not my fault."

Her grin widened. "Deal."

The bakery was smaller than I expected but also disarmingly cozy. Warm, honey-colored wood framed the walls, and sunlight poured through the front windows in soft, golden sheets. The air wrapped around me like a blanket, thick with cinnamon, sugar and that unmistakable buttery sweetness that all bakeries seemed to have.

"Hillary, this is Honey," Mimi said as we walked up to the counter. "Honey, this is Hillary Reyes. She is our head barista and my right-hand woman here at Bake My Day."

Hillary stood behind the counter with her hair in a messy bun, her apron already dusted with flour like she'd been born in it. When Mimi introduced her, her lips split in a wide, lopsided grin and I couldn't help but smile back. She looked so unbelievably pleased to be introduced that way and I knew the feeling. Mimi had a way of making you feel good without seemingly trying.

"Hi Honey! I'm glad I finally got to meet you," Hillary said as she waved. Her voice was sweet and a little soft. "I guess you're technically my boss too, so if I can help in any way, just let me know."

I shook my head. "No way. I'm just here to learn. I'm sure you are an amazing employee."

Mimi grinned at me before moving on to introduce Sophie, the part-time employee who couldn't have been older than twenty. She also gave me a shy wave but from behind the espresso machine. The steam hissed and curled around her in little foggy ribbons, and I waved back not wanting to disturb what she was doing.

Mimi took me around the rest of the bakery, walking from table to table introducing me to people who seemed to remember me even though we'd never met. It felt like I belonged here and that warmth hit somewhere deep and unguarded. In Chicago, people usually greeted me with professional polish or thin politeness. But here, it felt like stepping into a soft place I hadn't known I was missing.

"Come on," Mimi said, already heading toward the back. "I want you to help me with the croissants."

I blinked slowly, trying to understand what she was saying. "You want me to do what?"

She shot me a grin over her shoulder, her expression bright and teasing. "Trust me. You'll get it down in no time."

Of course I followed. I would've followed her into far more foolish situations than a bakery kitchen and that was saying something.

The back kitchen was surprisingly bright. Sun from the one large window on the back wall reflected off stainless steel, and jars of honey sitting on a shelf near it caught the light like glass jewels. The scents were stronger back here: butter melting somewhere and sugary fruit simmering low. Everything felt alive and warm. I loved it instantly.

"We're doing our peach-infused honey croissants

today," she said, pulling a tray of dough toward her. "Start by helping me laminate this."

I stared at the rectangle of dough like it had personally wronged me. "I work in PR, not pastry. Laminating means something very different to me."

"You'll be fine." She bumped her shoulder gently against mine. The contact was light and fleeting, but it jolted me more than it should have. "I'll teach you."

"Mimi…"

She grinned at me before her expression morphed into something that had my breath catching. "Come on. I know you can follow directions. I'll go easy on you."

I swallowed hard, my mouth suddenly dry. I found myself nodding and moving forward though my gaze remained on her. It took a moment to restart my brain and then I had to look at her hands to see what the hell she was doing to the dough. There was butter and then folding as she explained each step to me with more patience than I think I've ever had in my entire life.

We worked side by side, rolling dough, folding butter inside, pressing down and rolling again. The rhythm—press, fold, turn—settled into my bones. There was something soothing in the repetition and it grounded me in the moment. It tugged at buried memories: my mom in the kitchen, humming to herself, her hands confident as she kneaded dough while I watched from the stool beside her. I hadn't let myself think of that in years but somehow here with Mimi, the memory brought joy instead of pain. In this dough, I was finding more of my roots and a connection to the past I was always desperately missing.

"You're doing great," Mimi murmured, brushing a bit of flour from my wrist with her fingertip.

A spark leapt under my skin, bright enough I almost gasped. The kiss in the kitchen and my memory of how I'd come in the shower with Mimi's name on my lips had me clenching. This was not the time to think about how well she might fold and turn me. We were working.

Mimi reached for a small jar and twisted it open. "Here. You should try this."

She dipped a spoon in golden liquid before pulling it out and holding it out to me. For a second, I thought she might feed me—an irrational, ridiculous thought that still sent heat spiraling low in my stomach. Instead, she passed me the spoon, and I lifted it into my mouth.

My eyes flew open. "Oh my god."

The honey hit with a slow, rich warmth followed by a burst of peach across my tongue, bright and shockingly vivid. The honey was sweet in a way that felt like laughing as you ran as fast as you could with the sun dancing along your face. This wasn't just honey; it was an experience. When I opened my eyes and looked at her in wonder, her smile was wide.

"Right? Doesn't it taste perfect?" She asked with a knowing smile like she'd been waiting for exactly that reaction.

I swallowed, still a little breathless. "That's incredible."

"We drizzle it on the croissants right out of the oven." She stepped closer behind me, guiding my hands to the dough. Her fingers rested briefly over mine, soft and warm. "Here—finish this fold."

Our hands brushed. The touch was light and barely there, yet both of us froze. Her eyes lifted to mine, and suddenly she was so close I could feel her breath warming the skin near my jaw. The world narrowed until it was just her and the way her lips parted slightly like she was feeling the same tug I was. There was something electric and yet terrifyingly delicate at play here and I wasn't about to ignore how good it felt.

My heartbeat pounded in my ears as I leaned in. I could see Mimi doing the same as if we were two celestial bodies pulled together by gravity.

"Mimi?"

We jerked apart just as Hillary burst in, breathless. I could have groaned at being interrupted, but Hillary's expression was one of panic and it immediately put me on high alert.

"That guy is back."

Mimi's whole posture changed in an instant and immediately whoever the guy was, was on my shit list. "Fuck," she bit out before moving quickly. She wiped her hands on her apron, and I did the same as I followed her out of the kitchen.

We stepped out front, and sure enough, Charles stood there wearing that same glossy, rehearsed smile he'd flashed at me a couple days ago when I saw him in town.

"There you are," he said lightly as he looked at Mimi. When his eyes slid to me, they widened before his smile grew deeper. "Oh, perfect. I'm glad you're here as well, Ms. Parker. Have you given any thought about what we discussed?"

Mimi cut her eyes sharply to me. "What's he talking about?"

Charles shoved his hands in his pockets like he owned the room. "We spoke yesterday about a very generous offer that you must not have been privy to, Ms. Smith. Then again, since she's the last Parker here in town, she's the only one I really need to talk to."

Anger snapped up my spine—sharp and hot at how he spoke to Mimi. I felt her tense, and I took a step forward coming between her and him.

"And as I told you before, I'm not interested in talking to you about anything right now," I bit out. "Mimi is my partner and if I make any decisions, it will be after speaking with her."

"Well, Ms. Parker, I think it might be best if you ask her whether or not she has your best interests at heart given her family's background." I frowned at his words, not understanding what he was getting at. "Oh...you don't know? That's quite unfortunate. Ms. Smith, are you—"

"Get out," Mimi said, her voice deadly calm. I had never heard her speak to anyone that way and I looked over at her wondering what I was missing.

Charles chuckled, but the sound held no humor. "Ms. Parker, I truly believe we can make a deal that preserves your family's legacy while allowing you to return home."

"I have no desire to make any deals with you, Charles, and I am home." I took a step back to Mimi's side. "And I believe Ms. Smith asked you to leave."

His smile slowly morphed into a scowl. "You can't stop progress, Mimi. Hickory Springs is in a prime location to—"

"I don't want to hear it," Mimi cut him off. "Leave before I call the sheriff, and do not come back. Final warning."

Charles frowned, but the threat must have gotten

to him because he turned on his heel and marched to the door. He pushed it open and glanced once at me over his shoulder before walking outside and letting the door shut behind him. Revulsion crawled up the back of my throat. I had been around men like him, who wouldn't take no for an answer, and they always disgusted me and pissed me off in equal measure. Mimi didn't move until he disappeared down the sidewalk, her jaw locked so tight I could see the muscle working. There was a deep frown carved into her face but also concern as if she'd seen something that worried her deeply.

Chapter 12

Mimi

I told myself I wasn't going to think about Charles or worry about the way he'd said Honey's name like he was already calculating how to use her. I was heartened to hear Honey defend not only me but the Parker land and legacy she had inherited. Her disgust at Charles' words had not been subtle at all, instead written plain as day across her features. That had been a relief in more ways than one.

I knew I didn't have a claim on her feelings even with the way things were progressing between us. She could still decide to sell her shares of land and jet back off to Chicago and I wouldn't really have any recourse to stop her. Charles bringing up my family was a way for him to try to control the narrative, a narrative that I hadn't really been forthcoming about. Honey was smart and I knew she'd noted what he said. I needed to come out with it before she made her own deductions and came up with something worse.

She didn't owe me explanations, but I sure owed her some. My stomach twisted as I wiped down the tables, the rag dragging over wood polished so many times it had a soft, familiar sheen. My family name was common enough that nothing came of it when I moved to town years ago, but it still carried some weight. Money was one thing Bea, and I had argued over, especially as the farm's reserves shrank and she began selling off parcels to keep things going. I had offered to keep the farm afloat with my own money, but she'd refused. Loudly, in fact. I could have bought the farm out of debt and not batted an eye at the cost, but Bea was a proud woman and toward the end, she was so sick I felt like a bitch for bringing it up.

Maybe Honey will be different.

Finances wasn't a conversation that we'd had yet. I continued paying things and leaving the bills on the foyer table like I always had. Honey struck me as someone who defaulted to politeness even when she shouldn't, but I wondered how she would feel if I said I wanted to pay everything for the farm for now and the years to come? Would she think I was trying to buy my way into her heart? Would that be too much to over-come? I didn't doubt she would continue to deny

Charles a sale, especially with the way it looked like he made her skin crawl.

Something in my chest unclenched. Not entirely. But enough that I could breathe a little easier. We could make this work. I just needed to sit and talk to her and lay everything out on the table. I finished wiping down the table then turned and froze.

Honey stood beside Hillary at the counter, laughing at something Sophie said as she steamed milk. The sound of it floated across the bakery and slotted itself somewhere deep under my ribs. Honey was laughing like she felt at home here. She was plating pastries with careful precision, sliding a spatula under the fresh croissants Hillary had pulled from the warmer. Her movements were graceful in a quiet, intentional way—like she was used to working with her hands even if she didn't realize it. Her bright smile never waned as a customer thanked her like she'd personally baked the pastry she was handing over.

And it hit me low and warm. She looked...happy. The realization hit me in the chest. I liked her here in a way that felt dangerous to admit. I wanted her here in a way that felt dangerous to ignore. Before I could let myself drift too far into that feeling, the brittle hiss of small-town gossip floated from a couple tables over.

"Did you hear what that man said? Something about selling?"

"I did. And if Honey is back to sell Bea's place after all this time...well, that is a damn shame. I know Bea would be rolling over in her grave if she could hear it."

"She's an outsider now, anyway. Barely ever came back. I doubt she cares about this place the way Bea did."

My spine went tight before I started wiping at the same clean table, pretending I was too focused to hear them. It wasn't fair. They didn't know her. They didn't see the way Honey had teared up last night when she looked over pictures from Bea's closet. They never heard the way she'd whispered Bea's name like it hurt. They didn't see her truly trying to find her place in a town she barely remembered but still carried inside her like a bruise. Sometimes, small towns rarely cared about truth. They cared about narrative. And once a narrative caught fire, it was almost impossible to put out.

I inhaled slowly, forcing my shoulders to relax. I had to remind myself I couldn't snap at customers for being nosy and wrong. I was about to redirect myself toward the kitchen when my phone buzzed in my pocket. I pulled it out, confused when I saw Cassandra's name.

"Cass? What's up?"

"Mimi?" Her voice was breathless and filled with

alarm. "Something happened at the western apiary. I need you to come out here, right now."

My blood went cold. "What happened?"

"I'm not sure. You just need to get out here."

Cassandra never panicked. Not unless something was seriously wrong. I turned, already scanning for Honey without realizing I was doing it. She was sliding a fresh peach-honey croissant onto a plate, smiling shyly at a customer like she couldn't quite believe she deserved their gratitude. She looked soft and perfect like a future I wasn't supposed to imagine.

"Honey?" I called, my voice steadier than I felt.

She immediately looked up, reading my face in an instant. Concern flickered through her eyes. "Is everything okay?"

"Cassandra found something at the western apiary," I said, shaking my head. "I need to go check it out."

Her expression shifted, first to worry and then to something solid and firm. "Go. I've got things here."

"You sure?" I asked, even though I already knew her answer.

She nodded, stepping closer. "Go. I can find a ride back to the house if I need to."

Warmth spread through me, but I shoved it down before it could spread fully. I needed to focus on getting to Cassandra so I could figure out what was going on. I nodded sharply before grabbing my keys and heading for the door.

The western apiary was too damn quiet when I pulled up. Normally the hum of bees, moving from hive to flowers reached me before I even stepped out of the truck—a soft, living vibration that settled into my bones the second I got close. But today there was nothing. No bees drifting lazily between boxes. No darting guards buzzing near my hair. Just a thick, unnatural stillness that crawled over my skin.

Cassandra stood near the hives with her arms wrapped tight around herself, shoulders bunched, her braids were loose, falling over her shoulders. When she heard me get close, she looked up, her eyes burning with fury.

"What—" I started, stepping toward her, but my voice choked to a stop when I saw it.

The hives weren't just overturned. They weren't knocked slightly off-balance or nudged out of position like a hungry bear had gotten curious. They were fucking wrecked. Boxes were split clean down the middle like someone had taken an ax to them. Frames had been hurled across the dirt, some snapped in half. Sheets of wax comb were sliced and scattered. And honey was spilled everywhere—thick amber pools glistening in the sun, sticky and ruined. A few bees crawled aimlessly through the mess as if dazed, their wings vibrating weakly.

It was the type of carnage that only a person could make.

"Oh my god."

Cassandra swallowed hard. "I got here maybe ten minutes ago. I didn't see anything happen, but..." Her voice wobbled, then sharpened. "I did see a car driving away. It was a blue sedan with Georgia license plates, I think. I wasn't really paying attention. I just thought it was someone lost."

"This isn't your fault," I said immediately, stepping forward and putting a hand on her arm. Her muscles were trembling. "Hey. Look at me. You couldn't have known."

She pressed her lips together, eyes shiny with anger. Cassandra didn't cry easily, but this was a lot. This almost seemed personal. Animals scavenged. They knocked hives over to get at honey or brood. Animals didn't smash things in anger. This was deliberate sabotage.

The word stalked through my mind sticking to everything it touched. I crouched beside one of the frames, touching the splintered edge with the lightest pressure. It crumbled slightly, honey and wax sticking to my fingertips. My bees—my girls were scattered about dying or already gone. The colonies Bea had tended for years were scattered like trash and I hadn't been here to protect them.

A white-hot rush of rage shot through me so fast I nearly keeled over. I had to close my eyes just to breathe and stop myself from screaming. When I finally looked up, Cassandra was watching me with the same helpless fury. I forced some steadiness into my voice.

"Come on," I said quietly. "Let's see what we can salvage."

She nodded, wiping her forearm across her face. "Yeah. Okay."

We moved slowly through the wreckage. Some of the brood frames were still intact. A few of the queens might have survived. But the colonies were stressed, and it would take weeks—maybe even months—to stabilize things. If we even could.

The longer I worked, the more one thought kept circling. *Charles.* His name tasted bitter in the back of my mind like something old and rancid I'd accidentally bitten into. I didn't have proof that he might be involved in this. Not even close. There was just the too-convenient timing and the kind of greed that made men do ugly, irreversible things when they wanted control. He clearly wanted something here that we were standing in his way of.

I straightened slowly, staring at the ruined hives, my heart pounding so hard it hurt. I didn't care who he worked for or who he thought he could push around. Heaven would be the only one who could help him if he'd been the one to touch my bees.

Chapter 13

Honey

By the time Hillary dropped me off at the house, the late-afternoon sun had already slipped behind the trees, leaving the yard washed in soft mauves as the evening settled in. The air around me smelled like peaches and warm bread and if not for having already eaten my fill of croissants, I would've been starving because of it. The driveway was empty, and my stomach dipped when I realized Mimi wasn't back. I don't know when I had started expecting her to always be around, but I needed to get a hold of myself. She had things to do that didn't include babysitting me while I figured out my life.

"Are you sure you're going to be okay?" Hillary asked through her open window. "I can come in and sit with you if you want."

I smiled and waved her off. She really was sweet,

and she had quickly become one of my favorite people. "No, I'm fine. You go home before it gets too late."

"Okay," she replied. "But come back tomorrow, okay? I know you're the boss, but working with you was fun."

I laughed. "Mimi's the boss. I just show up from time to time," I replied. "But sure, I'll definitely come in."

I watched Hillary back her car down the driveway and waved before turning back to the house. I pushed open the screen door, wincing as it creaked loud enough to echo.

"Mimi?" I called out just in case though I wasn't surprised when only silence and the creaking of an old house answered me.

I locked the door behind me, before toeing off my shoes and tossing my purse on the table. There was a faint ache between my temples—a combination of being on my feet all day and worrying about the way Mimi had rushed off after that phone call. I hadn't heard the conversation, but I knew it had to be serious for Mimi to look as frantic as she did. Even Hillary said she'd never seen Mimi that way before.

My gaze flicked to the living room, where I'd dropped off boxes from the attic yesterday. They were stacked beside the old pine coffee table like a small wall of unresolved nostalgia.

"Well," I muttered to myself. "Guess it's just me and the memories tonight."

I walked into the living room and dropped down on the couch. I pulled the nearest box closer and coughed when dust puffed up in a little cloud, catching the last light spilling through the sheer curtains. The cardboard felt brittle, the edges softened from years of being ignored.

Inside was a stack of faded envelopes tied with twine. Beneath them, a mishmash of keepsakes—an old church bulletin, a couple of recipe cards in Bea's looping handwriting. I set them all to the side and then saw a broken chain necklace with a few dried rose petals trapped between two brittle napkins. Below that were more photos. There was a whole stack of them, rubber-banded together waiting to be viewed again.

For some reason, my fingers hesitated. I wanted to know more and yet every new discovery led to more questions. I didn't know how detectives ever solved cases when one question led to two more. Still, I couldn't stop now. Carefully, I slid the band free and lifted the stack.

The first photo on top caught me off guard. I knew that smile and dimple. It was my mom. She was maybe eighteen or nineteen, grinning as she stood on the front porch of a house I didn't recognize. Her hair was pulled back in the same ponytail I always sported, and

I felt my throat tighten as I peered down at her face, frozen in time.

"Mom..."

I brushed my thumb over the glossy edge. She looked happy and untouched by anything resembling the illness that came later and stole her away from me. I reached for another photo and saw her again, this time at a lake. Her arms were thrown around two girls her age, all of them squinting into the sun with the kind of joy you only have when you're young and the world hasn't broken you yet. I felt something warm unfurl in my chest. Then I froze. The next picture wasn't of her. It was of him.

My father was young, probably around the same age and wearing a smirk I hadn't ever seen on his face. He was perched on the bumper of an old pickup, holding a Coke bottle between his knees. He looked carefree. Mischievous, even. Like someone who flirted with trouble just because he could.

I wasn't sure how to feel. Seeing him like that stirred up a strange mixture of affection and resentment. My childhood with him hadn't been bad, not exactly, but it had been hollow in places. After Mom died, he had retreated into his work and only came up for air when it was time to scold me or tell me to push harder to be better. But here, in these frozen moments, he wasn't the man who shut down whenever I asked questions or the man who flinched at the sight of me looking or doing something that was too much like mom. He was just a boy, who was clearly happy and very in love.

I set his photo aside slowly, careful not to bend the corners. Another photo from the stack slipped free and fell face-down in my lap. I picked it up without thinking and then nearly stopped breathing altogether. I recognized the face smiling up at me, not from the past but from the present.

"Melanie?"

My word hung in the air as I stared at the young girl standing beside my mother. I blinked hard, sure I was misreading it. But no—that was definitely Melanie. Younger, sure, and with her hair longer, the curls wild as they framed her face. But it was her. Her smile was like my mom's, bright and unguarded. Their arms were linked like they were close.

Too close.

I stared at the image for several long seconds before flipping to the next. There was Melanie again. This time, she stood with both of my parents—dad on one side of mom and Melanie on the other. All three of them were leaning together, cheek-to-cheek, like they'd just shared a joke. They looked like friends, and something twisted in my gut.

"What the hell..." I whispered. With trembling

fingers, I pulled more photos from the pile. There were high school shots and backyard bonfires. I saw them together in more lake photos and dressed up at a dance that might have been homecoming or prom. There was always my mom in the center with my dad somewhere close. And Melanie was there, sometimes a shadow, sometimes right beside them both. I didn't understand what I was seeing until I found the wedding photos and my throat nearly closed.

There was my mother, radiant and laughing with her bouquet lifted high. There was my father, his eyes soft in a way I'd never seen in real life. And there, off to the side but unmistakably present, stood Melanie in a lavender bridesmaid dress. But she wasn't smiling. Not really. Her expression hovered somewhere between forced and...something tired or maybe resigned.

My hands shook as I turned the photo over. In Bea's looping scrawl it read:

Angeline + Joseph's wedding
Melanie—maid of honor

I stared until the words blurred. Maid of honor? My brain couldn't reconcile it. It didn't make sense given how Melanie always tried to push away my mom's name when it came up. Why had no one told me they'd been, what was clearly, very close friends? Why had neither of them ever mentioned this?

My chest tightened. I swallowed hard, reaching for

my phone before I could talk myself out of it. My father picked up on the second ring.

"Honey?" He said, sounding irritated already. "You know I hate when you—"

"Why are there pictures of Melanie with you and mom?"

A thick, heavy silence fell that stretched so long I had to pull the phone away from my ear to make sure the call hadn't dropped. I waited him out when normally I would rush to say something or apologize and change the subject. When he finally exhaled, it was sharp and more than a little defensive.

"Honey, I don't know why you're digging all that up."

"Because it's here," I said, my voice cracking with anger I didn't try to hide. "Because no one told me Melanie was part of your wedding party. Because she's in every picture like she mattered to mom."

"She did matter," he snapped and I couldn't stop my flinch. His voice dropped lower, the tone going in the way it always did when I got too close to asking questions he didn't want to answer. "But that's not the point. The point is that it doesn't matter anymore."

"It does matter," I insisted. "Tell me the truth. Were you cheating on mom with her? Is that why—"

"No," he cut in sharply. "I never cheated on your mother. Never. I loved her and I still do."

Tears pricked hot behind my eyes. "Then why—"

"When she died," he said, and for the first time, his voice softened and I heard the exhaustion there like it was layered over old wounds. "I needed help and Melanie was there. She understood it wasn't about love."

I sank back against the couch cushions, breath shaking. "God...dad. That's so fucked up."

"It was survival," he said. "Melanie and I talked about it, and it worked for us. She never worked again, and I had someone here to raise you without there being certain expectations."

The words sounded so callous and suddenly I felt something I hadn't expected.

Pity.

Melanie hadn't been some villain in my mind, but she hadn't been innocent either. Now, though, I saw something else. A girl who loved my mother. A woman who shouldered a grief that wasn't hers. She'd stepped into a broken home not because she wanted to replace anyone—but because someone had to.

I pressed my palm to my forehead. "You should've told me."

"There was nothing to tell," he snapped again, losing whatever softness he'd briefly held. "The past is the past. You move on from it, not dig it up like a dog with a damn bone."

I closed my eyes. "I *have* moved on, but moving on doesn't mean pretending the past never happened. I'm not getting rid of this part of myself just because it's inconvenient for you. There are good people here. There are pieces of mom here. I'm not walking away from it this time."

"You're a fool," he said flatly.

My breath left my lungs in one painful rush. "And mom would be disappointed in you."

The line went dead. I stared at the phone as my pulse roared in my ears. My hands trembled so badly I had to set it on the coffee table before I dropped it. I hadn't meant to be cruel, but the words were out there and as much as I didn't want to hurt him, they were true.

The room felt too quiet now as if the walls were holding their breath. I didn't know how long I sat there, shock and anger all swirling together in a storm I couldn't name. It wasn't until a soft creak sounded behind me that I realized I wasn't alone.

I turned and saw Mimi standing in the doorway. She looked worried and tired, but her eyes were fixed on me, gentle and too understanding. My heart lurched painfully.

"How much of that did you hear?" I whispered.

"Enough," she said quietly, stepping fully into the

room. She hesitated only a moment before asking, voice raw, "Do you really plan to stay here?"

There was no fear in her tone. Just a sort of fragile hope that had me standing and moving towards her. I nodded and had to swallow against the lump in my throat.

"Yeah. I do. I wanted to figure out who I was and I think I can only do that here." She took another step toward me. "I found another letter from Bea."

That made her stop short. "You did? What did it say?"

I reached into the box and pulled out the envelope I'd tucked beside me earlier. My fingers traced the cracked paper as I let myself hope.

"She told me," I said slowly, meeting Mimi's gaze. "To follow my heart and find my way home."

The relief that flashed across Mimi's face was followed by a longing so terrifyingly tender that I had no choice but to give in to this pull between us. Before I could breathe, she crossed the room in three quick steps, before cupping my face in her hands and kissing me. I fell into her like she was my first breath after I had been drowning. It felt like my body had been waiting for this exact moment and I didn't even know it.

Her mouth was soft and urgent, tasting faintly of honey and new beginnings. Her fingers slid into my hair, holding me with a kind of reverence that made my chest ache. The world outside faded. The boxes, old photos and the sting of my father's words dropped away until there was only this moment, only us.

When she finally pulled back, her forehead rested against mine, our breaths mingling.

"Don't leave," she whispered.

"I'm not going anywhere," I breathed back.

For the first time in years, the truth felt simple. I was home.

Chapter 14

Mimi

I tried to keep calm as I put away the final dish from dinner. Honey had been quieter than normal while we ate, though when she filled me in on what she had discovered, I understood why. Finding out your stepmother had been friends with your parents for at least most of their lives and no one told you, had to be a lot. I didn't even bother telling her about the mess with the hives. I didn't want her more stressed out than she already was.

Dinner had been a quiet affair, though being able to reach over and rub my thumb over the back of her hand had been a highlight. The smile she had gifted me with when I did was enough to keep my spirits out of the gutter. Cassandra and I had cleared most of the mess and we were already planning to rebuild things.

We weren't able to salvage the hives, but I would worry about that at a later date.

"What are you doing?"

Honey's voice surprised me, and I turned to look over my shoulder with a smile. "I'm just cleaning..." My voice trailed off when I saw what she was wearing. I knew she had gone to shower. I had done the same before dinner, but I had come back wearing a t-shirt and sweatpants while she was in the doorway with only a slip of silk adorning her. My mouth went dry as I looked her up and down. "What is the occasion?"

She shrugged. "Well, I thought that we could maybe take things further." She glanced up at me from beneath dark lashes. "Only if you're ready of course. I know we've only known each other for a few weeks, so I'm fine if—"

I cut her off before she could continue, moving across the room with determination and wrapping her in my arms. Her body molded to mine like two perfect puzzle pieces and I groaned when her mouth parted as soon as it met mine. She tasted spiced, like something exotic and intoxicating and I had to have more.

Hands gripped my hips as we moved, both of us occasionally drawing away to laugh when we hit a wall or a doorframe. By the time we fell onto her bed, my breath was hitching, and my shirt was somewhere on the floor. Our legs tangled together, and I shifted, pushing my pants down so I could feel as much of her skin against mine as possible. The silk camisole was in the way, and I bunched it up to her hip so I could run my palms against the skin of her hip.

"I wanted you as soon as I saw you," I whispered heatedly.

Honey chuckled and then groaned when I pressed my tongue against the underside of her chin, placing sucking kisses along her skin. "I think I accused you of trespassing."

"I like being accused of criminal activity apparently," I joked. "Really turns me on."

She shook her head and gripped my face bringing our lips together again. Our kisses were rough, both of us tasting from one another as we surged against each other. The bed creaked and groaned as we shifted and when we finally moved together with no fabric between us, I moaned softly into the skin of Honey's neck. Her own groan was buried in my hair even as her fingers gripped at my shoulders and pulled me on top of her.

Her legs fell open around me, and I pushed my hips down enjoying the way our bodies felt pressed this tightly. She was hot and the skin between her thighs damp already. "Were you getting started in the shower without me?" I asked as I propped myself up above her.

Honey grinned unrepentantly as she shrugged. "Wouldn't you like to know."

I arched a brow at her and pushed up until I was crouched on my knees between her spread thighs. "I would actually." When she frowned at me in confusion, I reached forward and took one of her hands in mine before moving it to her pussy. "I want to see how you touch yourself when you start without me."

Her eyes widened before they flared with heat. "You just want to watch me fuck myself."

"Yes," I answered simply, not denying it. Arousal shot through me with her blunt words.

Honey only paused for a moment before her fingers twitched and then moved. I lifted my hand, letting her proceed how she wanted. My gaze dropped to watch as she moved, her fingers inching up until they slid along the edge of her pussy lips only dipping in slightly like a tease.

"Are you trying to tease me or yourself?" I asked with a smirk.

She grinned. "Why not both?" Her fingers slid up further until they brushed over her engorged clit before she lifted them away. There was a string of slick that still connected them and without thinking, I reached out and gripped her wrist. She looked at me, a question on her face but I didn't speak. I leaned in, taking her fingers into my mouth and humming at the taste of her. I heard Honey's breath hitch and that was all the warning I had before her mouth met mine in a blaze of wet heat.

The kiss was wild, sending flares of heat through me until I felt my skin dampen with sweat. When I felt fingers brush against my own clit, I choked out a moan and fell back against her. Her hands were strong when she pulled my legs over hers spreading me over her hips.

"God, I love your curves," Honey hissed. Her hands spread over my sides as she shifted down below me. "I've been gagging to see them like this with no clothes. Fuck."

"Your mouth gets really dirty when you're turned on."

She grinned sharply. "You have no idea. But you will." I opened my mouth to respond, but before I could, two fingers slid deep inside me curling deliciously and making me groan.

"Fuck, you're so wet for me, Mimi," she whined the sound tearing through me.

I fell forward, one hand at her head to brace me up. The other, I buried in her hair gripping tightly when her fingers pumped so deep, I nearly couldn't breathe. I angled her head up and pressed kisses hard against her lips wanting to etch myself on her soul. When her fingers spread, pressing against the sensitive walls of my pussy, I cried out.

Honey played me like a tune she'd known all her life, fingers pumping and curling each time they retreated. Her thumb joined, toying with my clit like it had all the time and nowhere else to go. My thighs trembled and I gripped the back of her head not letting her go anywhere as I filled her mouth with my whimpers and moans. She wasn't silent, her lips hot as she spoke filth between my lips. The air between us grew hotter until with a final shocked sounding breath, my body clenched and I tumbled face first into ecstasy.

"There you go, baby," Honey whispered, her voice slowly coming back to me as my body came down from its high. "You come so fucking pretty. I want to make you look like that every day."

"You're more than welcome to," I gasped out as her fingers slowly slid from between the lips of my pussy. I fell to the side, our legs still entwined as I watched her bring her slick fingers to her mouth and suck them in. Her gaze never left me and I knew I wasn't letting her go. "Come here."

Honey tilted her head and looked at me until she realized what I wanted. She turned, bringing our lips together and I hummed when I tasted myself on her tongue. When we came up for air, I rested my forehead against hers, our breaths uneven.

"Fuck, you taste good," Honey said as she licked her lips. "Want to know how I taste?"

I smirked. "Oh I know how you taste."

"But don't you want to taste it from the source?"

My laughter was soft as I brushed my lips over hers. "If you want me to eat you out, all you have to do is ask."

Honey sucked her teeth before rolling her eyes with a smile. "Fine. Eat me out...please."

I pushed her onto her back before leaning back over her. "I would love to."

I sucked a trail of kisses from her neck down to her breasts, stopping to enjoy the way they filled my hands. Her nipples were tight little buds that I loved pressing my tongue against until she moaned. Honey's hands weren't idle, taking turns pressing against my skin or gripping me when I hit something that felt really good. By the time I brushed my nose over her clit, her breaths were coming out in soft whines.

I dug my fingers into her hips as I looked over her pussy. "You're fucking soaked. You spoil me."

"Don't tease."

"Never," I said softly before pulling her until her long legs slipped over my shoulders. I pressed soft kisses on her thighs. "I'm just trying to enjoy myself."

Honey's hips shifted. "Well, enjoy and stick your tongue in me already."

I snorted in amusement. "Note to self, that mouth gets dirty and disrespectful when you're naked." Still, I didn't make her wait. I had been wanting this for as long as she had.

The first taste of her was like ambrosia on my tongue. She was honey sweet and I gathered her slick on my tongue. "I dreamed about this. Dreamed about how you would feel on my tongue."

She moaned. "Is it good?"

"It's perfect," I hissed before diving back in for another hit. Was it possible to be drunk off someone's scent? I didn't know, but I felt like it.

When Honey's hips moved against me, I moved with them, letting the motion carry through as I ate from her ravenously. She was hot on my tongue and when her hands gripped the back of my head holding me in place against her cunt, I moaned and brought a hand down between my own legs until I could slide my own fingers between my pussy lips again. We moved together then, the bed creaking again and announcing our sex to the room. I didn't care. All I knew is I needed to know what it felt like to have her fall apart against me. I slipped one finger into her as I continued tonguing her pussy, loving the feeling.

"I'm so fucking close," Honey panted.

"Touch yourself," I breathed out as I slid a second

finger inside her. "Touch yourself for me. I want to feel you come."

She didn't hesitate, her free hand dropping down to squeeze her nipples and scrape nails down her stomach, the muscles jumping. When she touched her own clit, her sounds increased and I had to close my eyes as I felt my muscles tense again. I felt more than saw Honey come, her hips shooting up and her body trembling in my grip. When she fell back to the bed, I wheezed and came too, fire spreading through my nerves.

We laid there, our breathing syncing up as we took a moment. I leaned my head against her thigh enjoying the feeling of her leg trembling. When I looked up, Honey was looking down at me with a soft smile and I knew I would protect that smile for the rest of my life if she let me.

Chapter 15

Honey

6 months later...

A knock on the doorframe had me turning around. Mimi stood there, her hair creating a perfect halo around her face. Her expression was pinched and worried and I stood quickly wondering if everything was okay. It had only been six months since I decided to stay and we made our relationship official, but I could already read Mimi's expressions like I'd been privy to them since birth.

"What is it?" I asked, not sure if I could handle anything else after the call I'd had with my father earlier. "Is everything okay? Did something happen to the bees?"

She shook her head and snorted. "You care about those hives more than me now."

"I don't know about all that, but they are a big source of the farm's income." I gestured at the papers on my desk. "I've been working out some pitches that I want you to take a look at. I still have so much to learn about all this if I'm going to help market these things."

"'These things' she says," Mimi muttered though the smile on her face let me know she was just pretending to be difficult. I folded my arms and gave her a look.

"Are you just here to give me a hard time or was there something else?"

My question had her smile dimming and she glanced briefly over her shoulder. "Yeah. Melanie is here. She said she wanted to talk to you."

That gave me pause. Two months ago, when my father had finally broken our mutual silence and announced he and Melanie were divorcing, I thought that meant I would never have to speak to her again. I didn't know why she was here, but if she was hoping I would help her change my dad's mind, she had another thing coming. I didn't think my dad and I would ever have the perfect relationship. There was too much there that had gone wrong for too long for me to ever look at him without pain. But he was my dad, and despite it all, I couldn't hate him. I knew he loved my mom even if her loss had him pretending like he didn't.

"I can send her away and tell her you're busy if you want," Mimi continued when I didn't respond. I wanted to tell her to go ahead and do that, but I knew if I did, I would never get the closure I think I needed.

I shook my head and walked over to the doorway. "No, it's okay. I'll talk to her. I have some things to get off my chest as is and this might be the only time I have to do it."

She nodded as she looked at me. Her brown eyes held so much concern that I nearly collapsed into her. It was still so amazing to me to be cared for so utterly and completely. It made me want to wrap her in a cocoon and make sure she never felt anything but happiness and joy again.

"Why are you looking at me like that?" Mimi asked, refocusing my attention on her.

I smiled. "Because I love you." I pressed a soft peck to her lips. "That's all."

She snorted, but her grin was wide and pleased. "'That's all' she says. As if telling me you love me isn't the best thing ever." I laughed and shook my head at her antics but didn't hesitate to kiss her again. I had to force myself to back away when Mimi shifted just right and tried to deepen the kiss.

"Nope," I said, holding a hand against her cheek. "Raincheck for now otherwise I'll never figure out what she wants."

Mimi snorted but took a step back in clear agreement. "Alright, but if I hear yelling, I'm throwing water at her and calling my attack bees."

"You do that babe. I'll be back in a bit."

I walked to the front door and tried not to get distracted by how gorgeous the sky was at this time of early evening. It was still so breathtaking to me how beautiful this place was. When I stepped onto the porch, Melanie was already there standing to the right of me and looking more polished and put-together than I had expected. I let the door bang closed behind me and faced her.

"What are you doing here?"

She didn't bristle at my flat question. "I came to say goodbye."

"You didn't need to come all the way down here to do that," I pointed out. "My father said you two were getting a divorce."

"We are. It's been a long time coming honestly."

"True," I replied before looking away and down the drive. The car there wasn't one I recognized. Then again, she probably hadn't driven all the way from Chicago. Vaguely I wondered where she was headed and if she planned on going back.

"You know she is still his only love," I said, not bothering to look at her. Maybe it was wrong of me to say my feelings out loud, especially given what I'd learned, but after everything that had happened, I couldn't help myself. Finding out the truth—of how she and my father moved on after my mother's death—made me want to lash out for once instead of keeping my thoughts inside. "He never got over her."

Her continued silence finally spurred me to turn and look at her. I expected to see devastation and anger. What I didn't expect to see was understanding. Melanie gazed at me, her eyes shiny with unshed tears and yet she didn't yell at me the way I had thought was coming. She just seemed so...lost.

"Your father wasn't the only one who loved her, Honey." I frowned at her words.

"Of course he wasn't," I replied before gesturing around. "Everyone in town did. Every time someone mentions her, they talk about how good of a person she was."

Melanie nodded. "She was a great person," she said, not an ounce of sarcasm in her tone. "She was the best thing that ever came from this place...besides you."

Her words didn't make sense to me. For years she had acted as if the very mention of my mom was too much for her to bear, and now she was talking about how much everyone had loved her. It didn't make any sense, and I was through with being left out of the truth.

"Why are you saying this?" I asked, fists balled with frustration. "Why are you acting like you didn't hate the fact that my mother ever had me? Why are you acting like you cared about her?"

Melanie looked at me a moment longer before sighing and shaking her head. "Because I did." She looked away. "I loved your mother, Honey. I always had and even after her and your father...even after everything, I still do."

I blinked quickly, her words throwing me for a loop and leaving me standing there unmoored like a boat with no anchor. When she looked back at me, a tear slowly made its way down her cheek. I watched it, somehow understanding now the sincerity of her words. I could hear the pain in every tremble of her voice as she continued speaking.

"Your mom was...radiant. She had this uncanny ability to draw people in without really trying, and I was one of them." Melanie walked over to one of the rocking chairs and slowly sat. "When we first met, I had just moved to town with my grandmother, and I didn't know anyone. I walked into class that first day of school and I was terrified. But your mom was the first one who came up to me and invited me to play. I think I fell a little in love with her that day, and that love never went away."

I frowned and stared. "But..." My voice trailed off when I couldn't think of anything to say in return.

Melanie glanced down for a moment before fixing

me again with her gaze. "At first, I thought the feelings I had for her were platonic—hero worship for the person who took me in when I was lonely. But when we got older, the feelings never went away. And when she started dating your father, that's when I knew they were more than just friendship. I was jealous of him, not her—jealous that he caught her eye in a way I never could."

I leaned against the porch column as everything washed over me. I was having to reset everything I previously knew, and it was hard to do that in real time. Still, I couldn't help but want to know more. "Did you ever tell her?" I looked back at Melanie squarely. "Did she know that you loved her like that?"

"Sometimes I think she did. We kissed once—in high school on a dare. She always laughed about it afterwards, calling it her one real rebellion." Melanie shook her head as a small sad smile stretched her lips. "I don't think she ever realized that was my first kiss. I never told her and after, when I saw her kissing your father, I knew she would never feel the same way for me."

I sank down on the porch step then. My mind was blown. I had thought I figured everything out. I thought I knew the past now in a way that made sense to me, but I was realizing that there were some things that would just never be wrapped up in a neat box.

People were complicated and the past wasn't always clear after so much time had passed.

"Does my dad know?"

Melanie didn't answer for a moment. "He always did," she said finally. "I think that's what made it so easy for us to be together. We both loved your mother so wholly, that we thought we could get by sharing some part of her. But seeing you be so much like her in so many ways was hard on us both. In the end, I think we both resented one another for never truly being able to move on."

"You should," I said, surprising myself. "You should move on from him and me and try to find your own happiness. No one deserves to be stuck in the past. Not while you're still living."

I heard the rocking chair scrape against the porch and turned in time to see Melanie stand. She looked at me for a moment before nodding sharply. When she smiled, the sentiment didn't quite reach her eyes, but it still seemed more genuine than it had in a long time.

"I think you're right," she replied. Melanie walked toward me, not pausing as she descended the stairs, her shoes echoing hollowly on the wood. I watched her go, not sure what to say to comfort her or even if I wanted to at all. There was too much history there and I wasn't sure if it was history I wanted to hold on to. When she had gotten to the bottom of the stairs, she turned, her gaze looking past me and at the house. "I loved your mother, Honey. I loved her with everything I was."

I didn't say anything. There was nothing for me to say. My mother was part of me, and yet she was gone. The woman that had sat at the center of my father and Melanie's marriage was nowhere to be found. Not anymore.

She nodded, her smile falling before she turned and walked to her car. I watched as she started it, headlights turning on in the waning light of the sun. The silence was only broken up by the sound of tires over gravel as she backed out of the driveway and eventually disappeared from sight. I didn't think I would see her again outside of the pictures newly discovered in those attic boxes. The past had been uncovered, and it was more than I could have imagined. Still, I couldn't help but be glad for it. So many of my forgotten memories made sense in the wake of all I had learned. I could put together my family story a little easier now and it lifted a weight from my shoulders while settling me more into myself.

I didn't know how long I sat on the step staring out into the evening, but when I heard the door behind me open, I turned to find Mimi standing there, her gaze fixed on me. Her expression was curious, but she didn't ask anything. She simply walked over and held her hand out. I looked at it for a moment before lifting my own and letting her help me stand.

"I made dinner."

I smiled. "Thank you."

She held the door open, beckoning me back into the warmth of the house that had once again become my home. The familiar scent of lavender met me; a reminder of the legacy of love I had come from and the love that I had against all odds found for myself. I paused, turning to Mimi, marveling at the woman who had somehow helped me bridge the gap between my past and future. I reached down and grabbed her hand, enjoying how perfectly it fit in mine.

When I finally walked through the doorway, I didn't bother looking back

About Karmen Lee

Karmen Lee is an author of diverse and queer adult contemporary and steamy romance. She's a single mom living it up in Atlanta, Georgia with her kid, her cats, and humidity. When she's not carpooling or packing lunches, you can probably find her enjoying a glass of wine and dreaming up ways to show her readers a good time.

Sips of Her

Tastes of Him

Sweet Heat Holiday Novellas

Her Christmas Wish

Sipping & Swooning

Standalone Novellas

Finding Forever With You: A Second-Chance Novella

Only For The Night: A Sweet Temptations Novella

Changing Spaces: A Clover Hill Romance

www.ingramcontent.com/pod-product-compliance
Lightning Source LLC
Chambersburg PA
CBHW032018050726

47590CB00006B/2223